Clyde's hand slipped round Amanda's body and came to rest on the lush rounded globe of her right breast. As his palm cupped the full orb and his fingers played with the hardening nipple, a warm glow of delight spread through her entire body. She shivered as she felt his lips nibble the nape of her neck and then trace their way, in a tingling path of pleasure, down her spine into the small of her back.

Then, lower still beneath the delectable curves of her rounded buttocks, she felt another, even more delicious, sensation . . .

Exposure
In Paradise

Anonymous

First published in 1996
by HEADLINE BOOK PUBLISHING

A HEADLINE DELTA paperback

10 9 8 7 6 5 4 3 2 1

ISBN 0 7472 5285 8

Typeset at The Spartan Press Ltd,
Lymington, Hants

Printed and Bound in Great Britain by
Cox & Wyman Ltd, Reading, Berks

HEADLINE BOOK PUBLISHING
A division of Hodder Headline PLC
338 Euston Road
London NW1 2BH

Exposure In Paradise

Chapter One

The Paradise Country Club had certainly seen more than its fair share of ups and downs – both literally and figuratively – Amanda Redfern reflected dreamily.

From the run-down and somewhat seedy business which she had inherited some three years previously, the place had undergone an increasingly bizarre series of amorous adventures and carnal capers in which the only factor which had remained constant was the club's unswerving devotion to the pursuit of sexual pleasure.

In rapid succession, the establishment had been a rural retreat for cheating businessmen and their secretaries, a sex-rejuvenation clinic, a nudist camp and the throbbing hub of a series of the most wild and unbridled orgies.**

Now, under the new management team of Amanda and her two partners Andrew and Sally Baines, a pair of middle-aged but still inventive sexual swingers from the wild days of the Sixties, the Paradise was most definitely on the up. So much so, that it was rapidly acquiring the dubious reputation of being the most notorious knocking shop in the

**See 'Passion in Paradise', 'Scandal in Paradise' and 'Naked in Paradise'

country, with a regular clientele which reached deep into the very heart of the British establishment.

Life was exciting, and lived on something of a knife-edge. It seemed almost inevitable that, sooner or later, a major scandal would break which would rock the Paradise Country Club to its very foundations.

This discomforting reflection jolted Amanda further into full wakefulness, in turn provoking yet more gloomy thoughts. Suddenly, she had a terrible suspicion that such an event might have already occurred. With a sinking heart, she began to recall some of the wilder events of the previous night through the alcoholic haze of a full-blooded hangover.

Amanda was fully awake now, and conscious that she was in her own waterbed, in her own private quarters – and she was not alone. Rolling onto her back, she glanced sideways at her male companion, struggling to put a name to the sun-bronzed, golden-haired stranger who shared her pillow. Improbable as it seemed, the name Clyde sprang to mind. Clyde, from Australia. Clyde the apparently bottomless lager reservoir who had managed to convince her that she was a female kangaroo and that her cunt was a pouch into which he had to keep sticking his joey. As sex-games went, it was at least original, Amanda conceded.

The young man's eyes flickered open, a contented grin beginning to spread across his face. From his point of view, it was an extremely pleasant awakening, to find oneself in bed with a gorgeous young redhead with a face like a fallen angel and a pair of thirty-eight inch tits most men would kill for.

Amanda groaned. Clyde's handsome face clouded over, taking it as a personal affront. 'Last night I got the distinct impression that you quite liked me,' he complained miserably.

Amanda shook her head. 'Not you – everything else,' she muttered, as further memories of the evening's orgiastic activities began to surface in her consciousness. There was a pleading look in her eyes as she regarded him again.

'Tell me last night didn't happen,' she begged him.

Clyde shrugged. 'Last night didn't happen,' he said helpfully. It wasn't very convincing.

Amanda groaned again, rolling away from him back onto her side and burying her face in the pillow as if that could black out the lurid images rising in her mind. Taking the move as an open invitation, her young Australian companion moved in behind her, pressing himself into her back. Despite herself, and the fact that she still couldn't quite bring herself to believe she had gone to bed with a man named Clyde, Amanda found the feel of his hard masculine flesh against her body quite comforting. Less comforting, but still quite pleasant, was the sensation of something warm and soft being pressed between her rounded buttocks. Sensing what was coming, but not disposed to argue against it, Amanda made no move to wriggle away.

Clyde's arm slipped around her slim waist, his hand travelling up her flat stomach until it encountered the lush, rounded globe of her right breast. Having found its objective it rested there, the palm cupped around the soft flesh, two fingers pinching the small, firm nipple.

A warm glow of pleasure spread through Amanda's body as she felt Clyde's hot lips against her back, planting a series of quick, damp kisses down the highly erogenous valley between her shoulder-blades. She shivered as the feel of his lips gave way to the warm wetness of his tongue, tracing a saliva-coated path right down into the small of her back. Lower still, under the delicious cheeks of her arse, there was another sensation, equally erotic and stimulating.

What had been soft and merely warm was now burning hot and twitching gently against her flesh as it swelled into throbbing hardness. Amanda lifted one leg slightly, allowing Clyde's stiffening prick to slip between her thighs so that the meaty shaft pressed gently against the soft lips of her cunt. She clamped her legs back together, encasing the thick rod in the fleshy prison between her thighs and enjoying the sensation of the faint but regular pulsing of male power.

Clyde was gently massaging her breast now, kneading the pink bud of her nipple between finger and thumb until it, too, began to swell and throb with rising blood. Amanda purred with satisfaction, realising that the process of sexual arousal was now well under way and irreversible. She was relieved to know that sense was about to give way to the sensual, that physical pleasure would soon take her over completely, driving all negative thoughts from her mind. She wriggled her arse, allowing the thick shaft of Clyde's rampant cock to settle into the moist cleft of her cunt, its bulbous, swollen head in direct contact with the gently throbbing bud of her clitoris. A delicious tingling sensation rippled up through her belly, like a mild yet stimulating electric current.

It was a sensation which was most definitely more-ish, Amanda decided. She dropped her hand down over the flat plane of her belly, her fingers sliding through the soft, springy curls of her pubic hair. Encountering the smooth, rounded head of Clyde's fully erect cock protruding through her thighs, she pulled it up with her fingers, pressing it tighter against her sensitive clit and rolling it gently from side to side. The tingling sensation in her belly grew into a definite trembling as tiny pulsing waves of pleasure spread throughout her body.

Feeling her response, Clyde added his own contribution to Amanda's rising passion. Using only his stomach muscles, he began to pump very gently against her rounded buttocks, making his cock slide back and forwards along the crease of her rapidly moistening slit. Still using the heel of her hand to keep it pressed against her clitoris, Amanda's fingers slid back along its full length, tracing a line down the throbbing underside all the way to his swollen balls.

Clyde let out a gasp of pleasure. Amanda felt his hot breath against the nape of her neck, and shivered in erotic response. She was ready to move matters along now, feeling the bubbling secretions of lubricant welling up in her hot little fanny. Impulsively, she rolled away from him, letting his stiff cock slide out from between her legs. Turning first onto her stomach and then over again onto her back, she reached out to take it in her hand, grasping the thick stalk in a firm grip. With her free hand, she grabbed Clyde's wrist, spreading her legs slightly as she pulled him towards her and pushed his hand down between her burning thighs.

Clyde knew exactly what was expected of him. Taking a few seconds to stroke her silky pubis with the ball of his hand, he inched his fingers slowly forwards and down until they edged over the slight bump of her pubic mound and slid into the wet juiciness of her slit. Sinking three bunched fingers into the hot hole beyond, he began to rotate them slowly from side to side, his knuckles grinding against the super-sensitive clitoris which was now erect and twitching like a tiny cock.

Amanda was still holding tightly onto Clyde's throbbing prick. She began to rub it slowly up and down, thrilling to the feel of the swollen flesh pumping beneath the touch of her fingers, jerking in time to the pulsing of his hot blood. Clyde's body jerked convulsively as he thrust his hips forward, urging her to wank him more aggressively. Amanda got the message, tightening her grip upon his sturdy tool and starting to pump it up and down in a fast, regular rhythm, squeezing it at the same time. Clyde grunted appreciatively, stabbing his bunched fingers deeper into her brimming honeypot and craning his head forward to lay his face between her soft, beautiful breasts. Stretching out a hot tongue, he began to lick hungrily at the creamy flesh.

Content to enjoy the simple pleasures of mutual masturbation for a while, Amanda continued to pump his rigid cock until her wrist began to ache. Clyde's thrusting fingers had done their work now, already making a distinct sound as they thrashed around in a tunnel which was frothing with love-juice. Taking the next move on herself, Amanda pushed his hand away gently but firmly, pulling insistently on his prick to convey her needs.

Clyde was not slow in picking up the message. Eagerly, he clambered over her legs, settling himself down upon Amanda's knees. A dreamy look of pleasure spread across his handsome face as Amanda guided the swollen head of his cock towards the opening of her welcoming sheath. He moaned faintly with pleasure as she rubbed it briskly against her dripping cunt lips and clitoris, coating it with her own slippery secretions. Then, raising the weight of his body onto his arms, he adjusted his position until he was poised above her thighs, trembling slightly with anticipation as Amanda pushed his cock into the moist crevice between her soft labial lips.

As the first stiff inch of hot flesh settled into her juicy slit, Amanda's sexual floodgates burst open. She was hungry for his cock now, almost desperate to feel its throbbing length deep inside her belly. She arched her hips, thrusting her body upwards in a violent movement which would impale her upon his fleshy spike. The sensation of having his cock suddenly swallowed by her hot, liquid love-tunnel hit Clyde like an unexpected and numbing blow to the belly. Temporarily weakened, his arms seemed to turn to jelly and collapsed, letting the full weight of his body fall upon hers.

Amanda let out a little scream of triumph as Clyde's great prick rammed home like a pile-driver, powering its way smoothly along the well-lubricated shaft of her creamy love-tunnel until it met the constriction of her cervix. Her legs came up to wrap around his broad back, tightening in a vice-like grip to pull him down to her, merge his flesh with hers. Tensing and flexing the muscles of her stomach, she began to squeeze at his intruding cock like an electric milking machine, trying to suck it even deeper into the wet recesses of her ravenous cunt.

Somewhat restricted in movement by the constrictor-like embrace of her legs, Clyde could only pump his hips in short, stabbing movements which made his heavy balls slap against Amanda's smoothly rounded arse. The sensation was enough to draw a low moan of sensual pleasure from her lips. Her spine arched and went stiff, the lower half of her body rising from the bed to grind her hips into his.

Locked together in this position of total penetration, it seemed that little further movement was possible. They needed a bit of extra help, Clyde decided. Reaching up above Amanda's head, he grabbed hold of a pair of plump, soft pillows and dragged them down the bed, stuffing them under her buttocks. The hastily improvised ploy worked, the softness and resilience of the pillows allowing him a precious few inches of movement. He began the pumping motion of his hips again, making his stiff ramrod jerk and thrust inside her once again.

The support of the pillows also gave Amanda a chance to manoeuvre, and she seized upon it eagerly, rolling her arse gently from side to side. Together, the two movements seemed to merge into a single, fluid sensation which soon had them both gasping with sheer unadulterated pleasure. Clyde marvelled at the sensation of having his prick completely swallowed by Amanda's deep and juicy cunt, the very walls of which seemed to suck and massage his stiff flesh like some fantastic love-machine which had a life of its own. For her part, Amanda was blissfully aware that she was completely filled with cock, a mighty, meaty organ which throbbed and pulsed not only within her belly but within her very being.

She was so utterly fixated upon this single sensation that she failed to recognise the first warning ripple of her impending orgasm. Before she realised it, the secondary wave was already upon her, coursing up from the pit of her belly like an eruption, sending seismic shock-tremors through every other part of her body.

Clyde felt the waves emanating from her body. For a split second, he felt a great sense of disappointment, thinking that Amanda was about to come leaving him still unsatisfied. Then the sheer passion of her exploding orgasm swept him up in its strange power, washing him along in a lava-flow of liquid heat. His cock jerked and twitched, his swollen balls surging of their own accord, priming the final contraction which would send his own hot come spurting into Amanda's pulsing body. Grateful for this unexpected chance of release, he let himself go, heaving down against her cushioned buttocks with one final savage thrust as he shot his load.

Amanda's final yelp of pleasure coincided exactly with a knock on the bedroom door. Sally's familiar voice echoed into the room from the corridor outside.

'Amanda – it's me. Can I come in, or are you otherwise engaged?'

Amanda wriggled neatly from underneath Clyde's heavy body, sitting up in bed against the headboard.

'I'm otherwise engaged – but you can come in anyway.'

Clyde glanced sideways at her in disbelief. 'Jesus Christ, lady – don't you have any sort of privacy around this place?'

Amanda merely smiled, not bothering to answer him. It would have taken too long to explain the full degree of intimacy and lack of inhibition among the Paradise Club clique. When shared partners and group sex were commonplace, there seemed little point in being coy with each other. Unaware of this, the blond-haired Australian hastily pulled the duvet up to his chin as Sally sauntered casually into the bedroom.

Sally cast a quick, appraising glance over his handsome, sun-bronzed features before directing her attention to Amanda with a slightly envious look on her face.

'Ah, I did wonder what happened to this one,' she observed. 'I might have guessed you would have scored the best-looking hunk for the night. Any good, was he?'

Amanda shrugged carelessly. 'Not bad, actually – for an Australian. Size and stamina more than made up for any shortcomings in technique.'

Clyde's face was a picture. He looked bemused, slightly shocked and more than a little aggrieved at being discussed like a piece of meat on a butcher's hook.

His humiliation was not yet over, however. With deceptive speed, Sally snatched the duvet from his grasp and pulled it down to his feet in one smooth movement, fully exposing his naked body.

'Just thought I'd see what our friend from down under has down under,' she muttered absently to Amanda, her eyes firmly focused on the portion of his anatomy in question. A slight lifting of her eyebrows revealed that she was favourably impressed. Although flaccid, Clyde's cock was still reassuringly fat and well-proportioned, still glistening wetly with love-juice.

'Did you want something?' Amanda asked after a while, as Sally continued to ogle the young Australian's prick with undisguised appreciation.

Sally marshalled her attention again with some difficulty. 'Oh yes, Andrew wanted to see you,' she said, slightly absently. 'Some repercussions from last night, it seems.'

Amanda groaned again as the nightmare returned. The party which had turned into a wild orgy, the group sex session in the outdoor swimming pool, the police raid. That particular part of the previous night's fiasco was no doubt what the 'repercussions' were about.

Amanda dragged herself out of bed and over to the wardrobe, starting to dress. Sally, meanwhile, was doing the very opposite, neatly stripping off her blouse and allowing her huge, plump tits to swing free. Amanda gaped at her in astonishment. 'What the hell are you doing?' she demanded incredulously. 'I thought we were going to have a management meeting to discuss our problems.'

Sally was hardly listening. She moved towards the bed slowly and purposefully, licking her lips in anticipation of Clyde's muscular and athletic body. 'You and Andrew can handle it,' she said confidently. 'Right now I want to find out if you've left any life in our young friend's didgeridoo.'

There was little point in arguing, Amanda thought. Knowing Sally as she did, there was not much which could deter the woman from pursuing a course of action once she had set her heart on it. Especially if that course of action involved sucking a limp prick back into throbbing erection. She finished getting dressed as Sally dropped to her knees at the side of the bed and plunged her face into the young Australian's crotch.

Clyde was still too mind-blown to argue as Sally's hot and agile tongue snaked out to start licking Amanda's secretions from the side of his soft prick. 'Never look a gift mouth in the horse', a little voice whispered in the back of his mind. Abandoning himself to the mercy of a particularly carnal-minded nemesis, he lay back and made the most of the situation as Sally began stuffing his soft cock between her full lips with her fingers, slurping and gobbling upon it greedily.

Her cheeks bulged out as the tumescent flesh began to swell and stiffen in her mouth. Amanda decided not to stay around to watch. Leaving Sally single-mindedly devoted to her task, she made a discreet exit.

Chapter Two

Andrew was sitting in the breakfast room, drinking black coffee and looking distinctly the worse for wear. A large pile of morning newspapers cluttered the table in front of him. He looked up gloomily as Amanda walked in.

'Are we in trouble?' Amanda asked warily, reading the expression on his face.

Andrew forced a brave grin. 'I'm not sure,' he answered. 'But we're certainly in the news. Didn't Sally tell you all about it?'

Amanda shook her head. 'She couldn't say much at all. She had her mouth full at the time.' She did not elaborate, and Andrew didn't bother to pursue the matter.

Instead, he picked up one of the newspapers, holding it up so that Amanda could read the glaring headline. 'CABINET MINISTER IN MULTI-SEXUAL ORGY' it screamed out in huge black print. Andrew picked up another paper, opening it out on the table. 'POLICE RAID COUNTRY SIN-BIN'. Finally, he indicated the whole pile.

'They're all much the same. The media's closing in like a pack of wolves. The phone's been ringing all morning. I've had to leave it off the hook.'

Amanda tried to look at the situation from a positive

angle. 'They do say there's no such thing as bad publicity,' she said brightly.

Andrew looked unconvinced. 'They also said that the bloody Titanic was unsinkable,' he pointed out.

Amanda took the point. 'Perhaps he's just a very junior Cabinet Minister,' she suggested hopefully.

Andrew shook his head. 'Afraid not. Senior figure, in a highly sensitive position. The Opposition's already calling for resignations and threatening a vote of no confidence. Heads are going to roll, believe me. The bloody Government could even fall on this one.'

Amanda let out a long, deep sigh. 'Which one was he?' she asked.

'The guy in the French maid's outfit wearing purple lipstick – remember?' Andrew told her.

Amanda nodded morosely, beginning to remember it all.

It had all started out innocently enough – if any party at the Paradise Club could be called truly innocent. Just the usual crowd of cheating husbands, nymphomaniac wives, transvestites, good-time girls, homosexuals, lesbians, petty criminals and defrocked vicars who made up the club's regular clientele.

It was difficult to pinpoint the moment at which things began to get out of hand, although the first signs of possible trouble broke out around the outdoor swimming pool around midnight. Fuelled by the vast quantities of champagne which had been flowing all evening, some bright young thing came up with the inventive idea of a 'swim 'n' screw' relay race, in which the object of the game was for each contestant in turn to swim one length of the pool, complete a sexual act with a partner of his or her choice, and swim back to the shallow end.

Everything was going well enough until a drunken house-guest wandering around in the garden observed one of these couplings from a distance, assumed that someone was giving the kiss of life to a drowning victim and called for an ambulance on his mobile phone. The 999 call somehow got re-routed to the police and the local constabulary, in the form of a single, and fairly simple village Bobby, arrived on the premises shortly after half past twelve. After that, it was downhill all the way.

Looking back now, Amanda could see that it was her friend Bella who had caused most of the ensuing problems – although the woman could hardly be blamed either for her nymphomania or her particular weakness for men wearing uniforms. Nevertheless, if she had not stripped off the unfortunate copper's trousers and demanded to see the size of his truncheon, it was unlikely that he would have sought reinforcement by calling in the Vice Squad. They turned up in force at around one o'clock, by which time the party had already started to assume the proportions of a Babylonian orgy. Copulating couples lay everywhere, Bella was cantering around on the lawn with the naked policeman on her back and Freda the Swedish masseuse was delivering relief massage to three minor members of the peerage simultaneously in the sauna.

The daughter of a well-known television commentator stood on one of the bar tables and named twelve possible fathers of the child she was convinced she had conceived during the past three and a half hours. A clothes-swapping session was well under way and the titled patron of a leading international charity had discovered that after fifty-three years of normal life and four children he was really a closet transvestite.

Worried by the number of well-known faces and prominent people in the crowd, the Vice Squad went the whole hog and alerted the Special Branch, who descended on the club at three am. They sprang into action at once, making random arrests and accusing virtually everyone present of crimes ranging from exhibitionism to high treason. The second-in-command of the Vice Squad was discovered in a wardrobe, wearing only a ladies thirty-eight-inch D-cup bra and with a dildo up his bottom. A drunken under-secretary in the Ministry of Defence erected a hasty platform from beer crates dragged up from the cellars and began announcing a long list of all known homosexuals, wife-beaters and possible security risks in the War Office.

Amanda found herself grabbed by a burly Special Branch man, who dragged her into what he thought was an empty room for interrogation. Inside, Bella was just finishing off a blow-job on the last of the local cricket team and marking her score up on the wall in lipstick. She looked up from her labours to eye-up Amanda's escort greedily.

'Ooh, super – another one,' she muttered drunkenly, leaving her current stud lying on the bed and lurching across the room. She had pulled the man to the floor and started to unbuckle his belt before he quite realised what was happening.

'You can't do this to me – I'm Special Branch,' he snarled in protest, trying to struggle free from Bella's clutches.

'You're all special to me, darling,' the woman breathed huskily, sliding down his zipper. Her hand was inside his gaping fly within seconds, feverishly groping for its hidden treasure.

Amanda got out while the going was good, evading further arrest by the simple expedient of grabbing the first free and reasonably good-looking male and dragging him off to her private suite. That the young man's name had turned out to be Clyde was only a small price to pay for such a fortuitous escape. And that, as they say, more or less brought things up to date.

Amanda snapped back to the present, regarding Andrew anxiously. 'So what happens now? Do you think they'll bring any charges against us?'

Andrew shrugged doubtfully. 'Your guess is as good as mine, old girl, but personally I can't see there's much they can do at all. We're a private members' club, properly licenced and nobody was doing anything which wasn't of their own free will. They can't accuse us of running a whorehouse because no money changed hands, except over the bar. As far as I know, holding a wild party on private premises isn't a crime in itself.'

Amanda looked relieved. 'So you reckon we're in the clear?'

Andrew took a little time to consider everything carefully, finally nodding his head. 'My guess is that the authorities will just let things die down naturally, although I wouldn't be surprised if they don't try to sneak a couple of spies into the place for a while just to keep tabs on what's going on. I'd say our biggest problem is going to be coping with the media. It's an even bet that we're going to have the tabloids on our back for a few weeks at least.'

Amanda smiled confidently. 'Then we'll just give them what they want,' she announced.

It was a decision which she was later to regret.

Chapter Three

Miles Lansing, Managing Director of Milestone Films, had one simple and basic philosophy which dominated his day-to-day existence. Lifestyle was everything. It was not only what one owed to oneself as a reward for one's labours, it was also the yardstick by which others could measure, and envy, one's success.

So the designer clothes, the fast sports car and the prestigious and expensively furnished Kensington apartment were as much for business purposes as for personal enjoyment. The six-person bedroom jacuzzi, on the other hand, was usually solely for pleasure, and Miles made the most of it.

Today was slightly different, as the bubbling spa and the two naked and busty blondes which it currently contained were serving the dual purpose of both business and pleasure. Milestone was a small, but highly flexible film production company, able to turn its hand to several different projects, from documentaries for the major TV networks to commercials or even pop music videos. When none of this work was available, Miles also turned out short soft-core 'girlie' films. It was something he would have liked to do a lot more of, but the market for such fairly innocuous stuff was strictly limited. One day, he had frequently promised himself, he would achieve his secret ambition and produce a really big-feature hardcore porno movie. Something to rank alongside such classics as *'Deep Throat'*, or *'Behind The Green Door'*.

But for the moment, he contented himself with eyeing up the two naked girls in the jacuzzi with undisguised appreciation. They were both from a modelling agency he hadn't used before, and definitely a lot classier than some of the part-time strippogram scrubbers he was used to working with. Of the two, the one called Sam was most to his personal taste. With an oval, high-cheekboned face framed by long straight hair, her features had an almost classical beauty, whilst her body exuded pure and raw sex appeal. Just over six feet tall, and with a slim waist and gently flaring hips, the girl might easily have been a top catwalk model if it had not been for the size of her delectable tits. But at a good forty inches, the full, rounded and melon-shaped treasures gave the girl a slightly top-heavy appearance, and would have distorted the lines of any fashionable dress or costume.

The second girl, who called herself Melanie, was pert rather than conventionally pretty, and her fleshy body seemed almost dumpy in comparison to Sam's trim frame. But it was a pleasing plumpness, and the abundant curves of her well-rounded arse balanced her large, swelling breasts more or less perfectly. The overall image was of a bubbly, friendly, and flagrantly sexy character. Built for comfort, not for speed, as they used to say. Somehow, Miles could not help suspecting that Melanie would be the hotter of the pair when it got down to the nitty-gritty. It was a theory he fully intended to put to the test before the day was out. It was not often that Miles could mix business with pleasure, and he wasn't going to let a chance like this one slip away from him if he could possibly help it.

Sam looked up at him with a faintly mocking, almost teasing smile on her full lips.

'Well, are you going to stand there all day, or are we going to get down to some real business?' she demanded. The gleam in her big blue eyes left Miles in no doubt that the question held a most definite double entendre. It sounded extremely promising, he thought.

He glanced up at the bank of video monitors suspended from the ceiling before answering. Each one showed a picture of the jacuzzi and its occupants filmed from a different angle, and each was working perfectly. The entire bedroom suite, in fact, was wired up for half a dozen different video cameras like a small-scale studio. Using either manual settings or remote control, Miles could film anything which went on anywhere in the room, including the king-sized waterbed. It was a facility which could be used either for business purposes, as now, or for recording intimate encounters for personal enjoyment. Miles had a large library of such tapes, with which he would often amuse himself or entertain male friends.

Satisfied that everything was up and running, he returned his attention to Sam. There was nothing else he really needed to do now, except let the cameras automatically record all the action in the jacuzzi. Later, he could edit and splice the videotapes at his leisure, to put together a film which would be acceptable to its undemanding audience.

'Right, let's get down to it,' he told the waiting girl. 'Let's make a naughty little movie.'

Sam grinned up at him sexily. 'Aren't you going to join us?' she asked.

It was an open invitation, which Miles seriously considered for a moment, finally shaking his head somewhat regretfully. 'Later,' he promised, realising that he needed to shoot a fair bit of footage of the two girls together before he could afford to indulge himself. He was, after all, paying them both by the hour and his main priority for the day was profit not pleasure.

Sam looked disappointed. 'OK, so what do you want us to do?' she wanted to know.

Miles shrugged. 'Just do a few naughty-girl things together,' he suggested. 'You know the sort of thing the punters like. I take it neither of you object to a bit of simulated lesbian stuff?'

Sam shook her head. 'It's all right by me – just as long as it *is* faked. I like my sex straight.' She glanced across at Melanie. 'How about you?'

The girl grinned broadly. 'I like my cocks straight and my sex kinky,' she announced. 'Basically I swing both ways and enjoy anything that's going.'

It sounded like a pretty good formula for fun, Miles thought. Also not a bad basis for shooting a sex film. Blue movies were always so much more convincing if the participants were really enthusiastic. He gave both girls a thumbs-up sign. 'OK, let's do it.'

He retreated to the bed and sat down to direct the action as the two girls moved towards each other purposefully. Something about the determined glint in Melanie's eyes told him that detailed instructions were not going to be necessary.

As he had expected, the smaller girl quickly made all the action. Her lush, ripe breasts bobbing on the surface of the swirling water, she moved across the jacuzzi and draped her arms languidly over Sam's shoulders. Pressing forwards so that their wet bellies were glued together, she arched her back and began to rock her upper torso gently from side to side.

Miles licked his dry lips appreciatively at the sight of the two girls' glistening flesh rubbing together. There was a growing tightness in his trousers, and he was already starting to regret his earlier refusal to join in the fun. However, the decision had been made. Reminding himself that this was work and not play, he relieved himself by adjusting the position of his swelling cock to a more comfortable angle and forced himself to appreciate the unfolding action on a strictly business level.

Despite a slight initial stiffness, Sam was loosening up now and was beginning to enjoy the silky softness of Melanie's breasts sliding against her own. She reached down to the surface of the water, cupping her hands under the two generous mounds and lifting them up so that the erect and prominent red nipples jutted forwards like a pair of tiny pricks. This manoeuvre having made up for the difference in their two heights, she was able to guide them against her own hardening buds. Nipple to nipple, tip to tip, the two girls began to move their bodies sensuously together in unison, causing Melanie to let out a little whimper of delight.

She tightened her arms around Sam's neck, pressing her face down so that she could lick her slender throat. There was no objection from the taller girl. Taking this as an open invitation to go further, Melanie raised her head slightly, first kissing Sam's cheeks and finally moving to her slightly parted lips.

Watching all this with detached curiosity, Miles felt his body tensing with slight apprehension as the two girls' mouths met. He was aware that the moment was a delicate one, that Sam was about to face a moment of truth. There was no way of predicting how she might react.

The kiss, at first no more than friendly, quickly turned more passionate as Melanie became bolder. Squirming against Sam's lush body, she pressed closer until their two pairs of tits were a soft squashy mass. She probed between the girl's soft lips with the tip of her agile tongue, pressing against her teeth and seeking entrance.

This was crunch time, Miles thought, as the tall girl's body stiffened in protest. He fully expected her to break away abruptly from the passionate embrace at any second. Instead, the moment of resistance passed. Sam visibly relaxed, responding to Melanie's lovemaking by throwing her arms around the girl's waist, gripping her plump buttocks with clenched fingers and pulling her closer so that their pelvises ground together, Sam's lips parted, letting Melanie's tongue snake inside her mouth, licking along the soft wet insides of her lips and beyond her teeth.

Miles had a full-blooded, throbbing hard-on now. The sight of two beautiful girls making passionate love to each other was highly erotic in itself, but there was an added thrill in realising that he was witnessing Sam reacting to a lesbian encounter for perhaps the first time in her life. It was almost like watching a virgin being deflowered, he thought to himself.

There was no longer any doubt that Sam was not only responding, but was actually enjoying the experience. For a girl who had professed that she only took her sex straight, she had thrown away all inhibitions. Her own tongue was working frantically now, darting in and out of Melanie's mouth in a flood of mixed saliva. Opening her legs, she clawed at the girl's beautifully sculpted arse, pulling her between her thighs. Using the buoyancy of the water, she lifted the smaller girl up, rubbing her wet mat of pubic hair against her own.

For her part, Melanie was obviously doing what she loved best, Miles thought. Again, although she had declared herself to be bi-sexual, it was pretty clear that she tended more to lesbianism than to heterosexual sex. Miles doubted that she would display quite the same passion and dedication to lovemaking with a man – although he for one would be more than happy to put it to the test.

Just thinking about it made his stiff cock twitch, sending a powerful jolt of sexual energy from his aching balls into his very bones. His throbbing erection was physically painful now, and his mind reeled with sheer frustration. He stared at the two girls hungrily, as though trying to will one of them into inviting him to join in the fun. They seemed oblivious to his presence in the room, both now totally engrossed in the excitement of their passion.

Miles dropped his hand to the front of his trousers, stroking his aching cock beneath the material as if to soothe away the pain. It didn't really help. He looked over at the two naked bodies writhing against each other again, suddenly realising that both girls were totally beyond caring about anything else that went on in the room. Suddenly, it

seemed stupid to have any inhibitions about his own behaviour in the light of what the two girls were doing quite
openly and unashamedly in front of him. They probably
wouldn't even notice, Miles told himself, giving way to the
overpowering urge which had just come over him. He
unclipped his belt and slid down his fly zipper before
pulling his trousers down to his knees. Sliding his underpants down to join them, he released his huge swollen cock
to stand up like a fleshy flagpole.

He clasped his hand around the thick stalk of his quivering prick, gripping it tightly and feeling the whole shaft
throb anew at his touch. A mixture of the strangest thoughts
and emotions suddenly flooded his mind. Like any normal
adolescent, he had wanked frequently throughout his teenage years, yet it must be nearly twenty years since he had
jerked himself off, Miles reflected. This revelation raised
the question in his head – why? Why had he allowed a sense
of shame to inhibit him, make him feel awkward, even
guilty about touching his own prick? It seemed strange
now, almost wrong, that a man could lose touch with the
most intimate part of his own body.

Now, gripping the stiff tool in his fist, he felt a distinct
thrill of pleasure, as though meeting an old and dear friend
after a long parting. He had forgotten the feel of hot,
throbbing flesh against his palm, the sense of wonder at the
size and power of his own manhood. Settling himself into a
more comfortable position on the bed, Miles began to rub
his cock gently up and down as he feasted his eyes on the
two girls' erotic coupling.

Both girls had one hand under the surface of the water
now, and from the rapid movements of their shoulders it

was obvious that each of them had their fingers stuffed into each other's cunts and were frigging away with gusto.

Three wankers together, Miles thought, a wry smile crossing his face. It all seemed rather amusing. He continued to stroke away at his cock at a leisurely pace, more as a form of relaxation than chasing quick sexual release. The entire experience had an almost dreamlike quality, a sort of pleasurable detachment, as Miles derived his vicarious thrills from observing the girls' uninhibited lust.

It was not to last long. Sam noticed him first, and quickly drew Melanie's attention to the sight of Miles playing with his sturdy cock. Both girls looked suitably impressed, for even from a distance, Miles' prick was an awesome looking weapon. The thick shaft was a good eight inches long and ramrod straight, but it was the smoothly sculptured, circumcised head which looked particularly appealing. Swollen and bulbous, it had the exaggerated and almost symbolic appearance of a painstakingly hand-crafted oriental dildo, except that it glowed with the rich purple shade of living flesh.

Sam's green eyes glittered like a feral cat. 'Hell, Miles – surely you're not going to let a beautiful cock like that go to waste,' she called over, taunting him. 'Come on over and join us.'

Miles felt his heart quicken at the invitation. Having watched the two girls fondle each other's lush bodies with such enjoyment, the thought of sharing such a wealth of soft female flesh made him almost dizzy with excitement. Yet his initial urge to jump from the bed and throw himself into the foaming jacuzzi was tempered with a sense of restraint. The need to assert his male dominance rose in him. He was, after all, out-numbered two to one, and both girls had shown clear signs that they didn't really need a man to give them sexual pleasure. To make his role an important one, then, it seemed necessary to control the action on his terms, not theirs.

He remained lying on the bed, slowly stroking his rearing prick in a deliberately tantalising manner. He grinned at Sam, matching her teasing smile.

'Actually, I don't feel like getting wet,' he countered. 'Why don't you two come over here and join me instead?'

There was a brief moment in which he felt he might have overplayed his hand and lost his chance. Melanie looked positively against the idea, and even Sam's face showed a certain degree of hesitation. She looked at him doubtfully for a few seconds, then glanced aside at Melanie, an unspoken question in her eyes.

Then, much to Miles' relief, both girls began to clamber out of the jacuzzi. With Sam very much in the lead, they scampered, dripping, across the carpet towards him.

The water mattress squelched and heaved like a storm at sea as the two girls threw themselves onto the huge bed, one on either side of him. Sam glanced down at his trousers crumpled around his knees with a disapproving look on her pretty face. Reaching down, she began to pull them off completely as Melanie started to unpick the buttons of his shirt.

Miles was still clutching his stiff cock as the girls quickly stripped him naked. Sam shot him another reproving glance. Taking him firmly by the wrist, she lifted his hand away, revealing the proud tool in all its masculine glory. She stretched out her fingers and touched it gently, tracing her perfectly manicured nails slowly and lovingly up its full length, from the base of the shaft to the glowing bulge of the swollen helmet.

Miles felt his prick twitch violently at her touch, and a fresh wave of electrical tingles rippled through his body. His breath rasped in his throat as the girl's slender fingers coiled slowly around the thick stalk, exerting loving, almost reverent pressure. Laying the balls of her fingertips over the throbbing vein on the softer underside, she squeezed gently in time with his pulsing blood.

Melanie was also keen to explore the tactile pleasures of his more than adequate cock. She raised one finger to her mouth, coating it with saliva against her wet tongue. Reaching down again, she slid her slippery fingertip around the shiny smoothness of the purple helmet, coaxing a tiny bubble of pre-come to ooze from the tiny slit at the top. Scooping it up, Melanie returned her finger to her mouth, sucking off the clear liquid like a humming bird would suck nectar. Disposing of the tasty treat, she licked her lips and returned her fingers to his prick, stroking it gently as Sam continued to squeeze at the base.

Miles shuddered at the delicious sensation of having two different hands caressing his cock. He knew the two girls were teasing him, and the aching feeling in his balls was becoming an actual pain, but this exquisite agony only heightened the pleasure. They would soon tire of just playing with him, he knew, and then the game could begin in earnest. He had no idea what form it might eventually take, but anticipation alone was like a powerful aphrodisiac, charging his whole body with latent sexual power.

The two girls seemed equally unsure about how the sexual threesome should develop. They glanced at each other uncertainly as they continued to stroke Miles' great cock, as if trying to communicate telepathically. Slowly, but inexorably, the atmosphere around the bed seemed to crackle with sexual tension.

It was Sam, perhaps the most sexually aggressive of the trio, who broke the temporary impasse. With a final squeeze, she released Miles' cock, looking first at him and then at Melanie with a devilish gleam in her eyes.

'Well, I think we both agree it's a terrific cock, Miles – but what are you going to do with it?'

Suddenly put in the hot seat, Miles was momentarily at a loss for words. Feeling rather foolish, he covered his embarrassment by throwing the problem straight back in the girl's lap.

'I rather thought you were going to come up with some suggestions,' he ventured.

Sam grinned, turning her attention to Melanie. 'Looks like it's all down to us,' she murmured. 'So, with one prick between us – do you want to fuck it or suck it?'

Melanie gave a lazy, uncaring shrug. 'You're calling the shots so you choose,' she said, in a slightly bored tone. 'Like I said – I can get my kicks any way that's going.'

Sam thought for a moment, finally treating Melanie and Miles to another one of her suggestive grins.

'Well we can't all fuck – so let's all suck,' she suggested. 'And if I'm calling the shots, I choose cock, at least to start with.'

It was time for action, not words. Sam set about putting her plan into action, knocking Melanie's hand roughly away from Miles' quivering prick and quickly re-establishing her own grip. Squeezing it tightly, she pulled it into an upright position as she adjusted her position on the bed.

Melanie got the idea as Sam twisted round until she lay on her side, her head resting on Miles' thighs and her body stretched horizontally across the bed. She moved herself around on the bed, taking up the same sideways position but fitting her body into the third side of an almost perfect triangle. Wriggling into the final position, Melanie buried her head between Sam's legs and thrust her pelvis provocatively towards Miles' face.

With the rules of the game thus laid out in detail, the players could begin. Sam's golden tresses tickled the soft insides of Miles' thighs as she nuzzled into his crotch, her soft warm lips pressed against the base of his cock. Delicately, like a cat lapping up cream, she began to lick at it with the very tip of her tongue, sending little shivers of pleasure vibrating down into his bursting balls.

It was time to make the next connection, Miles realised. He craned his neck forward, pushing his face into the soft and springy mass of Melanie's pubic hair. The smell of pure woman, the very essence of femininity, flooded his senses as his nose slid into the moist crease of her smooth little slit. Sticking out his tongue, Miles probed between the plump and soft labial lips, licking the rim of the tasty honeypot concealed beneath. Lapping to and fro along the full length of the girl's juicy slit, he curled his tongue into a tight, prick-shaped tube and stabbed it repeatedly against the quivering little button of her clitoris.

Melanie sighed deeply, her body squirming with satisfaction as she fine-tuned her own position in the triangle.

Plunging her head between Sam's thighs, she pressed her mouth flat against the girl's cunt and began to shake her head sideways, using her lips and teeth to prise open its fleshy portals.

Sam groaned as Melanie's stiff tongue slid into her dripping love-shaft, reaming it with a rasping, scouring motion which lapped up the flowing juices as fast as they could seep out. Sucking and slurping, she set about enjoying Sam's cunt as though it were some exotic fruit to be savoured, making little animal grunts of pleasure as she swallowed down each delicious drop.

Miles felt Sam's hot tongue gliding lazily up the shaft of his prick towards the swollen tip. Then her lush lips were easing over the top of the smooth helmet, until she held the entire dome in her mouth. His tongue still probing Melanie's juicy labia, he jerked his hips, sending the full length of his cock sliding into Sam's wet and welcoming mouth.

The sexual configuration was complete now, the circuit fully wired. Like the closing of a magic circle at some pagan ritual, this final connection seemed to release some strange energy source, which surged through the three bodies in a throbbing wave of sexual power. Each sucking and being sucked, the three participants set about their lustful business with feverish abandon. Mouth to cunt, mouth to cunt, mouth to cock. Sexual juices and saliva mixed together into a potent froth as the trio of naked bodies thrashed and writhed upon the undulating water-bed like some weird, multi-limbed and mythical beast.

Miles felt his stomach tense as Sam took his cock deep in her throat, pressing the shaft with her lips, rolling her agile tongue around its head and sides. His face was hot and wet with Melanie's copious juices, his brain racing with excitement. The two sensations at either end of his body seemed to come together somewhere in the pit of his belly, where they met and clashed in an explosion of opposing forces. He began to tremble violently, overcome with the heady passion of it all. Somewhere deep in a colder, more rational part of his mind, he realised that he was the weak link in the chain, that he was powerless to control or hold off his impending orgasm. There was a momentary feeling of guilt, quickly swept away by the urgency of his need for release. Miles let himself go as Sam sucked and lapped feverishly at his throbbing cock, drawing up his boiling juices as though from a deep underground well.

Sam let out a choking sob as Miles thrust convulsively against her face, driving his aching cock deep into her throat. She pulled away, momentarily, gasping for air before plunging her mouth back over the quivering rod, sucking and squeezing at it hungrily as it began to spurt a full load of come into the back of her throat. She rolled the savoury emission round in her mouth and over her tongue before swallowing it in a series of slow, small gulps.

Miles continued to thrust his curled tongue in and out of Melanie's delicious love-shaft, but the fire was gone from his loins and it was only a token act. His guts felt drained and empty, and he could feel the slow death of his own prick as its life-sustaining blood drained away and the stiffness of passion turned to the limpness of satisfaction. Suddenly, he felt foolish and strangely vulnerable.

The telephone shrilled. With a feeling of relief, Miles

lifted his face from Melanie's sopping cunt and pulled his soft cock from between Sam's lips. He sat up, swinging his legs over the side of the bed as he prepared to answer his timely caller. Hardly had he risen from the bed than Sam and Melanie filled his place in the magic circle again. Twisting themselves round into a classic *soixante-neuf* position, the two girls happily sucked at each other's cunts as Miles strolled across the bedroom to the telephone.

He was pleased to identify his caller as John Standish, one of the chief commissioning agents for one of the major commercial television channels. Good friends as well as business associates, John made sure that he placed a regular supply of work in the way of Milestone Films.

Miles greeted him warmly. 'Hi, John – what can I do for you?'

John got straight to the point. 'Look, Miles, I don't know whether you're aware of it, but we're currently commissioning a new series called "The X-Zone". The idea is a series of forty-five minute documentaries on Britain's sex industry, planned for the late night/early morning slot. I wondered if you'd be interested?'

Miles jumped at the invitation enthusiastically. 'Does a whore fuck? Of course I'm interested. What's the angle?'

'There's something I read in the papers this morning,' John went on, 'some place called the Paradise Country Club where apparently all sorts of naughty things go on. It occurred to me that you might charm your way in with the management and get a small crew in to film the sexual shenanigans.'

Miles grinned broadly to himself. It sounded good, and

was getting better by the second. He spoke with assured confidence. 'John, you just got yourself a documentary,' he said firmly.

Chapter Four

Miles eased the white BMW through the huge wrought-iron gates which marked the perimeter of the Paradise Country Club grounds and up the long gravel drive towards the main building.

Appraising the gothic facade of what had once been a grand old stately home through the windscreen, he found himself quite impressed, although it did not look anything like he had envisaged. Perhaps because of all the media reports on the place he had studied carefully for the past few days, he had been half-expecting some sleazy looking and run-down house, perhaps with a garish neon sign erected outside. Instead, he saw a well-restored historic building, set in landscaped and immaculately maintained grounds, and obvious signs that a sizeable amount of money had been spent on the place in recent months. Newly surfaced tennis courts, a large and tastefully built outdoor swimming pool and the lush greens of what looked to be an excellent nine-hole golf course all gave an impression of opulence and respectability.

Perhaps it even looked *too* respectable for his purposes, he thought, remembering the brief he had been given. Seeing the place through the eyes of a film-maker, he had to admit that it would look good on camera, but the image did not seem in keeping with a rural den of vice and iniquity. Strangely, it all reminded him of the setting for one of those old naturist films of the nineteen-sixties which had been considered outrageously sexy for their time. Lots of bouncing tits and wobbling buttock shots of naked young lovelies playing things like volleyball and tennis, cut with the occasional ultra-daring view of a flaccid and drooping male penis. The entire image, of course, had been so coy and so self-consciously filmed for the sake of 'arty' effect, that the end results had been about as sexy as a nun's flannel nightie.

The thought that he might have to turn out something similar in the nineteen-nineties made Miles shudder with horror. He brought the car to a halt outside the huge front door and climbed out, feeling distinctly depressed.

The up-side was that he might not be filming at all, he thought, trying to cheer himself up. The owners could easily refuse to co-operate point-blank, in which case he would simply have to go back to John Standish and request a different assignment. Everything really depended on this first contact.

He had come straight down without telephoning for an appointment, counting on the strength of his personality and the warmth of personal contact to overcome any initial resistance. His researchers had done their work well, establishing that the Paradise Club was owned by a young woman of colourful background, in partnership with a couple of former staff. That much sounded promising to Miles, who prided himself on a certain degree of success with young women – and, if the rumours he had heard were correct, then Amanda Redfern was a particularly delectable example of her gender. With a bit of luck, he might just get a lot more than just forty-five minutes of film.

The heavy oak door was open, and slightly ajar. Pausing only to straighten his tie and sweep his fingers through his luxuriant dark hair, Miles stepped over the portal and strolled into the reception area, from which a faint buzzing sound was emanating.

There was an attractive young redhead seated behind the reception desk, who seemed to be totally engrossed in her own little world. She did not look up as Miles approached the desk, and it was obvious that she had not heard him come in above the loud buzzing noise which Miles could now tell was coming from behind the desk, being apparently obsessed with something between her legs. Miles took advantage of the girl's concentration to appraise her more closely.

She was more than just attractive, he thought, as he came closer. Although he could not see her face clearly, her figure alone announced that she was an absolute stunner. Under her crisply starched white blouse, a pair of huge, beautifully rounded breasts flared inwards to a tight little waist. The film-maker in him surfaced again, and in his mind's eye, Miles could already see those delicious tits shot in naked close-up and projected in gloriously magnified technicolour upon a giant screen.

It became obvious now what the girl was doing. Her shapely legs spread wide apart and her panties pulled down to her ankles, she was easing the frustrating boredom of her lonely job by stroking a battery-powered vibrator lazily in and out of her auburn-fringed cunt. Miles suddenly felt a little awkward, like a Peeping Tom who has been caught in the act. Silently stepping back a few paces until the girl's activities were masked by the top of the reception desk once again, he gave a short warning cough.

The girl looked up with a startled expression on her face, and Miles could see that she was every bit as beautiful as he had imagined. Huge, mischievous and slightly slanting eyes held more than a hint of sexual devilment, and her full, soft mouth spoke of a highly passionate nature. Amazingly, she did not betray any embarrassment. Apart from that initial moment of surprise, the girl's eyes met his with a cool, level and friendly smile. The sound of the vibrator snapped off abruptly. Moving her chair in slightly under cover of the reception desk, the girl recovered her aplomb in an instant and was at once charming and briskly efficient.

'Can I help you?' she enquired politely.

Miles made an effort to keep a perfectly straight face, responding to the girl at a similar level. It was not easy, having witnessed her previous activity, or being acutely aware that the area all around the desk reeked of the faint but unmistakeable aroma of cunt juices. However, he managed to disguise his grin as no more than a friendly smile.

'I'd rather like to see the management, if I may,' he said rather formally. 'I don't have an appointment, but I assumed this would be a fairly quiet time for you.'

The girl nodded in agreement. 'Yes, there's not usually much going on around here in the daytime. It's only at night when things really get going.' She reached for the phone. 'I'm sure someone will be free to see you. Who shall I say is calling?'

'Miles Lansing,' Miles told her. 'Of Milestone Films.'

The girl's eyes flickered with sudden interest at this piece of information. She regarded Miles in a new light. He was not merely a young man who was reasonably attractive, she realised now. He was a young film producer who was reasonably attractive. There was a whole world of difference. She hastily finished making the call and returned her attention to him. Discreetly reaching down under cover of the desk to pull up her panties, she stood up and leaned over towards Miles, holding out her hand.

'My name's Shelley, by the way,' she announced brightly. 'I used to be a glamour model, but I work here as a receptionist at the moment.'

Miles grinned to himself, recognising the sudden change of attitude for what it was. He had seen it a thousand times before, but it still never failed to amuse him. The look on Shelley's face was as plain as if she had suddenly held up a large printed sign, on which were written the words I WANT TO BE IN THE MOVIES AND YOU CAN SLEEP WITH ME IF YOU LIKE. It was an invitation he rarely turned down.

For the moment, though, Miles chose to just play along. Attractive though she was, Shelley was only a bit player in the game, and not a great deal of use to him other than as a potential ally. Amanda Redfern was the woman he really needed to charm, and until he had won her over it would not pay to show too much interest in anyone else.

On the other hand, there was no point in losing Shelley's interest either, he reflected. He accepted the girl's proffered handshake, eyeing her up with the look of admiration she was obviously expecting.

'Yes, I can quite believe you would do well in glamour modelling,' he murmured. 'You certainly look extremely photogenic.'

It was a little bit of bait, not quite a promise, but Shelley accepted it eagerly. Her eyes sparkled. Drawing in her breath and stiffening her body, she treated Miles to the best possible view of her straining breasts. 'Perhaps I could pose for you sometime,' she suggested. 'In case you ever need extras, or anything like that.'

It was time to back off, Miles thought, nodding politely. 'Yes, that might be a good idea,' he murmured. 'I'll have to think about it.'

Shelley looked slightly disappointed, but accepted the discreet put-down gracefully. With a final smile which was full of sexual promise, she returned to her role of efficient but slightly detached receptionist. There were a few moments of awkward silence before Andrew and Sally stepped out into the reception area.

It was Miles' turn to be slightly disappointed as he saw the couple. Sally was attractive enough, in a somewhat blowsy sort of way, but clearly the wrong side of forty and too old to be Amanda Redfern. Miles already had them pegged as the two minority partners even before Andrew introduced himself.

'Mr Lansing?' he asked somewhat warily. 'I'm Andrew Baines and this is my wife, Sally. We're Miss Redfern's business partners in the Paradise Country Club. What can we do for you?'

Miles had been hoping to go directly to the top, but he tried not to let that show. He shook Andrew's hand warmly, forcing a friendly smile. 'Actually, it's probably something which you would all like to discuss together,' he said cautiously. 'Is Miss Redfern available?'

Andrew shook his head. 'Unfortunately Miss Redfern had to go into London on business,' he told him. 'She probably won't be back until tomorrow. Perhaps if you could outline your business to me I could discuss it with her when she returns.'

Miles hesitated, caught on the hop. He racked his brains quickly, thinking on his feet and trying to figure out the best course of action. He was aware that Andrew was regarding him with undisguised suspicion, even veiled hostility. Sally, on the other hand, was most definitely eyeing him up, appraising his youthful body with an almost hungry expression on her face.

There was something about Andrew and Sally Baines, Miles remembered vaguely. Some little rumour or snippet of information which his researchers had reported to him and which he had thought might possibly provide some sort of bargaining chip. It surfaced, at last, in his mind. The pair were reputed to be sexual swingers of the old school, he remembered now. Still heavily into sex-games, swap parties and group gropes. The germ of an emergency plan began to form inside his head. Perhaps there was some way of playing Sally off against her husband, use her obvious sexual interest to counterbalance his antagonism. First of all, though, he needed to play for time.

'Look, I've got a much better idea,' Miles announced, impulsively. 'Why don't I book in here for the night and treat myself to a well-deserved break? That way I can take a little time to look around the place, and be here to see Miss Redfern when she arrives back tomorrow.' Before Andrew could offer any argument, he turned his most sexy smile on Sally. 'I take it you do have some spare rooms? I mean, they're not all reserved for members or anything like that?'

Shelley saw her chance and jumped in quickly, beating Sally to an answer. She too had a vested interest in encouraging Miles Lansing to spend a night in the Paradise. She would not be the first or the last girl to successfully screw her way into the movie business.

'Of course we've got rooms,' she announced eagerly. 'With every possible comfort for a tired businessman like yourself.' To make sure that Miles hadn't missed the point, she lifted her fingers to the two top buttons of her blouse, deftly unpicking them and exposing the creamy swell of her magnificent cleavage.

Andrew frowned, feeling vaguely as though he had been somehow outwitted. 'So what is your business, Mr Lansing?' he pressed, trying to re-assert himself.

Miles decided on a half-truth. His plan was still only half-baked, and he had no choice but to play things by ear. He produced a visiting card from his top pocket, handing it to Andrew for his inspection.

'I run a small independent film production company,' Miles announced, 'and basically I'm interested in using this place as the location for a feature which I've just been commissioned to produce.' He glanced discreetly at Sally, as he spoke, noting her reaction to this information. As he had fully expected, it was similar to Shelley's. So far so good, Miles thought to himself with a sense of satisfaction. He returned his attention to Andrew, who was reading the card with an uncertain look on his face.

'Well, if that's all settled, perhaps I'd better check in,' Miles suggested, consolidating his position quickly before the man could put in any objections.

Shelley was already reaching for the registration book and switching on her most disarming smile. Sally moved quickly, determined not to let the younger girl snatch the advantage a second time. She moved in on Miles like a protective mother hen, grasping his arm firmly. 'Oh, no rush,' she gushed. 'Why don't I take you for a quick look round our facilities, and you can register later.'

It was an awkward moment for Miles. Sally was laying it on a bit thick, and he wasn't sure how Andrew was going to react. Finally, however, the man glanced at his wife, caught the hungry, pleading look in her eyes and aquiesced with a faint shrug of his shoulders. He and Sally had long ago made a simple pact when it came to sexual digressions. Each partner had complete freedom to choose, quite independent of whether that choice was approved of by the other. He might not like Miles Lansing, or even trust him, but it was obvious that Sally fancied him. It was a purely sexual thing, and nothing whatsoever to do with the deep and enduring feelings they shared with each other. In all their wild and varied erotic experiments and adventures, whether singly or together, there had never been a moment of envy or mistrust, for the extra participants had been only objects of pleasure and not personalities. A succession of cunts and cocks, but never real people. That was the simple secret which had made their bizarre marriage work over the years.

With this in mind, Andrew faced Miles directly, no longer seeing him as a man. He was simply a thing which

Sally wanted to use for a quick and quite meaningless sexual thrill. He could not begrudge her that, any more than he would object to her masturbating in the privacy of her own bath. None of this, of course, was reflected in the brisk and businesslike way in which he addressed Miles.

'Alright, I'll leave you in my wife's capable hands, Mr Lansing. I do have rather a lot of paperwork to catch up on. Perhaps I'll see you later tonight and we can have a talk over a drink or something.'

Miles nodded. 'Yes, I hope so,' he said, and really meant it. Somehow, he was already getting the impression that both Sally and Shelley intended chasing him round for the rest of the night and he might need Andrew as a form of protection. Perhaps more to the point, he still had distinct reservations about getting involved with anyone before he had a chance to get to Amanda – although a business partner's wife was possibly one step up the sexual ladder from a receptionist.

For the moment, however, he had little choice in the matter. Shelley was still regarding him through smouldering, lascivious eyes and Sally clutched at his arm like a predator holding onto a fresh kill. Caught between a rock and a hard place, as the Americans say, he could only go with the flow. Quite apart from an obviously elevated position in the pecking order, perhaps Sally was the least threatening option, Miles thought.

It was a totally wrong assumption, of course – but then Miles was a total innocent when it came to the ways of the Paradise Club. He allowed Sally to start leading him away down the corridor, unaware that he was about to become a very quick learner.

'I think we'll start with a visit to the massage and treatment suite,' Sally announced in an apparently casual and harmless tone. 'Then I can introduce you to Freda.'

Chapter Five

Sally dragged Miles towards the massage room purposefully, feeling her cunt tingle with anticipation of what was to
come. That she would shortly be enjoying the pleasures of
the young film-maker's cock was guaranteed, almost inevitable – for Freda's sexual magic had never yet been known to
fail.

Sally felt absolutely no qualms or sense of shame about
using the Swedish masseuse as a sexual primer. She had
done it a dozen times before, and one tended to stick with a
proven and successful formula. And that formula was
simple – just introduce any normal man to the Junoesque
beauty and he had a raging hard-on in seconds. One glimpse
of her huge, creamy-fleshed tits had him trembling with
desire, and ready to ram his stiff cock into the first hole
which presented itself.

The tricky bit, of course, was to be the right hole, in the
right place, and at the right time – but Sally had long since
got this down to a fine art. It usually entailed sharing at least
some of the spoils with Freda, but that only added to the
fun.

Reaching the treatment room, Sally pushed open the door
without knocking, knowing that she would be welcome

whatever the girl was doing. Like every other regular at the Paradise Club, Freda had long ago forgotten the notion of privacy, and accepted the simple fact that nobody walked into a room unless they were fully prepared to share in whatever was going on or wanted to start something. The fact that these somethings were invariably of a sexual nature was almost co-incidental.

So seeing Sally was a pleasure in itself. Freda was already bored and frustrated, having had a quiet and deeply disappointing day. Two elderly female clients whose scrawny bodies held no pleasure at all, and a single man seeking relief massage who had shot his load into her hand the second she touched his dick. The appearance of Sally, therefore, was the highlight of her day so far, and held out at least the promise of fondling soft, resilient flesh. The fact that she had a man in tow was a real bonus.

Miles could only gawp at the female Amazon as Sally dragged him into the room. Like many men before him, the first sight of Freda's stupendous body was an experience which dried saliva in the mouth, caused balls to contract and click together like castanets.

As usual, the blonde Swede was naked from the waist up. A practical girl, Freda was well aware that her massive breasts did not take kindly to any form of restraint and the majority of her clients were impressed at the sight of them. Male or female, Freda's magnificent frontal development evoked either lust or envy – and she was more than happy with either emotion. For just as her tits were her greatest asset, they were also the source of her greatest pride and pleasure. She massaged and played with them constantly, both to maintain their firm tautness and to enjoy the sensation. Indeed, she had been doing exactly this before Sally and Miles had entered the room – which was why her large red nipples stood out like a pair of ripe tayberries and why Miles was now staring at them so fixedly.

'Freda – this is Mr Lansing,' Sally said, making the introductions. 'He's staying with us for a night of rest and relaxation, so I thought we'd start by letting you relieve his tension.'

Miles groaned inwardly as the Swedish girl turned to face him, her eyes beginning to glow with anticipation. The sinking feeling in his belly was matched only by the rising sensation in his prick as he realised that he was a doomed man, that his best intentions were about to go to the wall. His resolution to remain sexually uninvolved was now a lost cause, of that he had no doubts. Too late, he realised that he would probably have been better off entrusting himself to Shelley's clutches. She, at least, might have taken a polite 'no' for an answer and gone back to the consolation of her vibrator. With Sally, he had no chance, he saw that now. He was enough of a manipulator himself to see exactly what her game-plan was. Coming to the massage room had been no accident, but rather a deliberate ploy on her part. A born-again eunuch would have been hard-pressed to resist the sexual magnetism of the formidable Freda – and Miles had few illusions about who would take over the leading role once the now inevitable sex-games got going.

There was a brief moment in which he might have been able to save himself by turning away and making a run for it, but it passed away as Freda advanced upon him and he felt the familiar delicious agony of his throbbing cock trying to burst out through his trousers. Knowing he was beaten,

Miles surrendered himself as the Swedish girl's glorious tits wobbled towards his face.

A firm hand descended to his fly, outlining the bulging outline of his trapped cock and squeezing it experimentally. Freda clucked sympathetically, half-turning her head to address Sally.

'Ja – is much tension,' she muttered in her peculiar broken English. 'Is very stiff, our Mr Lansing. Much needing massage, I think.'

Without another word she threw one arm around Miles' back, slipping her hand under his armpit. Releasing his cock, she thrust her other hand under his knees and lifted him bodily into the air like a life-sized rag doll. Miles lay in her sturdy arms helplessly as the Swedish giantess carried him across the room and dumped him down unceremoniously onto the massage table. With briskly efficient fingers, she released his belt and zipper and pulled his trousers off with one smooth tug. His shoes and socks followed in quick succession and Freda began picking at the buttons of his shirt.

Sally scurried across the room to stand over the table, eager to see what sort of a treasure the Swedish girl had unearthed. So far Miles was still something of an unknown quantity and she had no idea what he had to offer in the sexual equipment department. Indeed, up to the time she had noticed the promising bulge in his trousers, she hadn't even known if he was straight or gay. One heard so many lurid tales about people in the movie business, it appeared to be a fairly hit or miss affair, and she had been quite prepared for a bitter let-down.

She was not disappointed. Sally breathed a sigh of relief

as she feasted her eyes on the healthy state of Miles' magnificent erection. Still totally mesmerised by Freda's creamy, fruit-tipped tits, he had lost all control over his prick, which now reared up like a stiff ramrod, throbbing erratically with a life of its own.

Freda had also been pleasantly surprised. Most of her clients tended to be middle-aged businessmen who had let their bodies go to seed. Miles was different. Not only was he the right side of thirty-five, he was well-built, if a trifle on the short side, and had obviously looked after himself. Though not particularly muscular, his flesh was firm and well-moulded around his bones, and there wasn't a trace of flab to be seen. For a girl who had made almost a fetish out of physical culture, the naked body of Miles Lansing was a minor treat in itself. The size of his quivering cock was just the icing on the cake, and she might get around to enjoying that a little later. For now, she was content to explore other parts of his firm young body.

Licking her lips with anticipation, Freda stepped on the frame of the massage table and lifted herself up, swinging one long and muscular leg over Miles' recumbent form.

For a moment, Miles was convinced she was going to mount him there and then and the muscles of his stomach tensed in readiness. Instead, Freda's hand reached for his dancing cock, pulled it down flat between his legs and eased herself over it, settling herself down on his upper belly. Released again, Miles felt his cock spring back up into an upright position, tucking itself neatly into the cleft between Freda's firm, rounded buttocks. It was a highly erotic sensation, made even more exciting by the feel of her hot, damp cunt pressed against his belly. He shuddered with pleasure as the girl leaned forward, sliding her hands up over his hairy chest towards his shoulders. Using her thumbs and fingers, she began a firm but surprisingly soothing massage, seeking out hidden muscles and areas of tension which Miles didn't even know he had. It felt unexpectedly good.

Miles had never really thought much about men having erogenous zones, even less about the possibility that his own body was positively crawling with them. Now, however, he had not only discovered their existence, he was acutely aware that Freda had an uncanny knack for finding them. His entire body vibrated with little shock-waves of sensual delight as the girl's skilled and nimble fingers seemed to probe beneath his skin and trip off a series of hidden pleasure-switches. All the separate little spasms began to close up together, until they finally merged into a single bolt of energy which felt both icy-cold and red-hot at the same time. It seared down the entire length of his spine, finally exploding out through his pelvis and shooting up his prick, which danced like a candle in the wind.

It was like a homing signal to Sally, who had been standing back and merely admiring the aesthetic beauty of the rigid cock apparently growing from Freda's gorgeously sculpted rump. Now, seeing it twitch as though beckoning to her, she was unable to resist any longer. Sucking against the sides of her cheeks and rolling the resultant saliva around in her mouth, she jumped forward and threw herself over the bottom end of the massage table between Miles' legs.

Miles heard the slurping, liquid sound of Sally's lips working only milliseconds before he felt their hot wetness clamping over the end of his rigid cock. He shuddered anew as she sank her mouth greedily upon its full length, constricting the muscles of her throat and gullet to hold it in a soft, fleshy grip.

It was a cock almost perfectly built for sucking, Sally decided, as the smooth circumcised head slid effortlessly into her throat. Taking a deep breath in through her nose, she gulped in a precious few more centimetres and held it there, rolling her head gently from side to side. She sucked on it until she could hold her breath no longer, then reluctantly had to come up for fresh air.

Miles let out a low, undulating moan as Sally pulled her head back, letting her waggling tongue rasp over the pulsing underside of his prick. She licked and kissed the swollen dome for a few seconds then dived again, swallowing the juicy treat until her lips were buried in the wiry bush of his pubic hair.

Miles felt quite light-headed, almost delirious with sensual pleasure. Freda's enchanted fingers had moved up around the sides of his neck now, and had discovered a whole new collection of sensitive pleasure spots behind his ears. Her body rocked slowly to and fro as she kneaded his flesh, making her huge breasts swing pendulously. Momentarily, as he drew in a deep and shuddering gasp for air, Miles felt the stiff buds of the girl's delicious-looking nipples brush against the hairs on his chest with a delicate, featherlight touch.

It was the final sensation which pushed him over the edge. With a sense of careless abandon, he capitulated absolutely and was no longer just a passive participant in the game. With a deep sigh, he reached up and clutched the two fleshy globes in his hands, pulling them towards his face.

Straining his head upwards, he began to suck upon each fruity nipple in turn, savouring the feel and the taste of them between his lips.

Freda let out a little gurgle of delight as Miles squeezed and fondled her soft breasts with increasing passion. She shook her upper torso gently from side to side, making them jiggle in his grasp. His hungry mouth followed the sensuous sideways passage of her nipples, determined not to let them go. When the pressure of his lips alone was no longer strong enough to hold them in place, Miles seized upon one quivering teat with his teeth, nibbling at it gently as he lashed the burning tip with the end of his tongue.

Freda's body stiffened as a wave of sensuous pleasure tore through her. Although Miles did not realise it, he had done the one thing which could raise the Swedish girl to the burning limits of desire in moments, for her highly sensitive nipples were the most erogenous part of her body, acting like hair-triggers. Miles felt a hot and wet flush against the flesh of his belly and realised that Freda's cunt had discharged a spurt of pre-come which would put many a woman's full orgasm to shame.

Freda rolled her arse wildly, grinding her pelvis down and smearing the silky juices across his stomach. With the area thus lubricated, she was able to start up a rocking motion, arching her muscular back so that the fleshy lips of her cunt made the maximum contact with Miles' stomach. Pumping her hips up and down, she slid up and down from his belly-button to his breastbone, riding him like a monkey on a stick.

There was no pretence of massage any more. Far from delivering pleasure to Miles, Freda was now unashamedly using his body to find her own. As far as Miles was concerned, he was more than happy to let the big Swede use him as a masturbatory object, for he was still getting as much sexual pleasure as he could handle from Sally, who was rapidly proving the best fellatrice he had ever encountered. In his considerable experience, surprisingly few women were capable of delivering a really satisfying blow-job, most only managing to make the act a pleasant but strictly temporary digression before normal sex.

It was all to do with attitude, Miles supposed. How a woman looked at oral sex. The majority regarded it as some sort of favour to the man, an offering of selfless debasement for which he ought to feel grateful. Very few genuinely enjoyed sucking cock as an act in itself, and that was what made the difference.

Sally's total dedication to the job was spectacularly different. The attention she was lavishing upon his prick was so intense that Miles was doubtful about which of them was actually receiving the greatest pleasure. Her mouth was a hot, wet, ravenous and sucking hole; her thick lips a fleshy vice which clamped around the fat stalk of his prick like the most juicy of cunts.

Freda had moved up onto his chest now, rubbing her wet cunt frantically against the hardness of his ribcage. No longer restricted by her weight upon his belly, Miles was able to move the lower part of his body more freely. He took advantage of the opportunity to flex his stomach muscles, jabbing his hips downwards to ram his cock even deeper into Sally's sucking mouth. The woman responded with a low grunt of animal pleasure, coiling her tongue back in her throat to act as a soft cushion for the thrusting intruder and pressing her lips even more firmly around its meaty shaft.

Miles knew that he was about to come, and the heady anticipation of release was mixed with the faintest twinge of anxiety. Faced with his imminent orgasm, Miles had absolutely no idea what would happen in the immediate aftermath.

Only one thing was for sure – any moment now he was going to have a spent prick and two extremely charged up and unsatisfied women on his hands. It was a daunting prospect, and he wasn't at all sure how he was going to handle the situation. Whilst he prided himself that he wasn't a 'slam, bang, thank you ma'am' sort of man, Miles was honest enough with himself to know his limitations. After coming, he invariably needed at least twenty minutes before he could raise a decent hard-on again. Under normal circumstances, with a single woman, this was not a problem. With the time in between filled with a bit of casual love-play, or even a shared cigarette, he could usually pace himself to fuck all night if need be, ensuring that his female partner was not disappointed. Coping with a large Swedish nymphomaniac and an oversexed middle-aged swinger was a different matter entirely.

However, the problem was already largely academic. Miles could feel his prick throbbing violently in Sally's hot mouth, and the familiar tingling sensation in his balls which told him he was about to come. There was no way he could hold it back. Surrendering himself to the inevitable, Miles accepted the savage joy of release and pumped his creamy discharge deep into Sally's hungry throat.

Gulping down the first savoury mouthful, Sally pulled her head back slowly and closed her lips into a tight pout around the head of his cock, licking the slit at the top with her agile tongue as though seeking dessert. Then, plunging her mouth back down the full length of the softening shaft, she pressed her lips tight and drew back again, squeezing it out like a tube of toothpaste. Finally, she let it plop out of her mouth and stood up, running her tongue dreamily over her lips and panting like an over-excited puppy.

She gazed down at Miles' deflating prick hopefully for several moments, finally shrugging her shoulders in resignation. Her vain hope that Miles might have turned out to be some sort of superstud had been mainly wishful thinking, so she was not really disappointed. It was, after all, purely her own fault that his proud cock was reduced to its present sorry state. If she hadn't been so greedy, if she didn't enjoy sucking a fat prick quite so much, then she would have left something over for seconds.

But the situation was not completely hopeless, she thought philosophically. Miles might be out of the running, but there was always Freda and her secret weapon. It was not as good as the real thing, but it did the job almost as efficiently.

She turned her attention to the Swedish girl, who was still furiously humping herself on Miles' chest in a froth of love-juice. She was putting a lot of effort into it, but didn't appear to be gaining much satisfaction. Tapping the girl on the shoulder to gain her attention, Sally pointed down at Miles' dead prick with a wry grin on her face.

'I seem to have sucked the life out of him, Freda. Maybe this is a job for Dick Double-Up.'

Freda ceased her grinding movements abruptly. A knowing grin spread over her face. She nodded. 'Ja, I think you right,' she muttered, beginning to climb down from the massage table.

Miles was a little confused. He had been expecting, even fearing, two rampant and sexually cheated women venting their frustration on him. Instead, it appeared that he had been let off the hook, that neither of them really cared. He found himself wondering who the hell this Dick Double-Up was as Sally began to strip off her clothes and Freda moved across the massage room to rummage in one of the equipment cupboards.

His curiosity was soon satisfied as Freda pulled a squat, tubular object out of the cupboard and started back across the room. As she neared, Miles could see that the object she held in her hand was a dildo, although it was like no other dildo he had ever seen, or even heard of. Fascinated, he propped himself up on his elbows and stared at the object more closely.

It was, in fact, two dildoes joined together back to back as it were. Or, to be more precise, one large double-ended imitation prick. Just over a foot long, and with a circumference of about five inches, Dick Double-Up was a beautifully sculptured piece of sexual equipment which had obviously been designed and moulded with loving care. Miles assumed it to be a product peculiar to the modern Swedish sex industry, which would explain why he had never seen anything like it before. In fact, this assumption was wrong, the device actually being of Oriental origins and based on a design which went back over three centuries.

Totally intrigued now, Miles watched with interest as Freda carried the object proudly over to the now naked Sally and presented it for her inspection and approval. Both women stroked the knobbled shaft lovingly, their eyes glittering.

Sally sank down to the massage room floor, sitting up-right and spreading out her outstretched legs. Freda went down to join her, taking up a position directly facing her and shuffling forward on her arse until their two pairs of legs overlapped. Then, each woman lifting one leg over that of her opposite partner, they arranged themselves like two pairs of interlocked scissors and squirmed closer until they sat no more than ten or twelve inches apart and their two pairs of breasts were touching, nipple to nipple.

Holding Dick Double-Up with the air of a High Priestess with a sacred ceremonial object, Freda lowered it reverently between her legs. Then, with slow deliberate care, she inserted one bulbous, shaped end into her cunt, twirled it round a couple of times to lubricate it with her flowing juices and then slid it halfway up her shaft with a blissful look of satisfaction on her face.

The visual effect was totally bizarre, Miles thought. With the flesh-coloured device rammed into position, Freda became an instant hermaphrodite. Miles blinked at the sight of a huge-breasted girl with a stiff six-inch prick rearing from the bushy blonde hair of her cunt. As he watched, Freda waggled the protrusion enticingly towards Sally, who began to wriggle her arse to move nearer.

Delicately, Sally eased the imitation prick between her own fleshy labial lips and pushed herself forward onto its full length. Dick Double-Up was completely swallowed now, one half in either woman yet totally in both at the same time. Though essentially simple, the device had achieved an almost magical transformation. Two women had become two creatures of both sexes – each of them equipped with a cock and able to fuck each other. Squirming even closer together, until their two cunts were pressed wetly together and their breasts mashed into a soft, amorphous mass, Freda and Sally began to make love.

Miles continued to be engrossed, his only detached thought being one of regret that he couldn't preserve the amazing sight on film. At that moment, he would happily have emptied his bank account for the loan of a camcorder, or sold his soul in exchange for a full lighting and film crew. Even a cheap Polaroid might have been worth a tenner.

Freda and Sally were getting into their stride now, developing a rhythmic movement between their two bodies which delivered the maximum amount of stimulation to each. It was obviously a technique which they had practiced many times before, Miles realised, for the simulated copulation would have looked incredibly awkward between two inexperienced participants. Freda and Sally, on the other hand, were obviously totally attuned to one another. There was a sensuous, fluid grace to the way in which they thrust and writhed against each other, each clenching their pelvic muscles at different times so as to grip the false prick and withdraw it from their partner's cunt then slide it back in again. It obviously took considerable effort, for both women were now grunting heavily – both from exertion and from pleasure. Their faces were flushed, their mouths hanging slackly open as each of them climbed slowly up towards a sexual plateau which hovered just short of orgasm.

It was clear that their little game could go on for ages, Miles realised. Without the limiting factor of a man's need for release, they could probably keep each other stimulated for hours and only end the love-play when they tired of it. His prick had begun to stiffen into life again at the erotic sight, but somehow Miles knew that there was no longer a role for him to play. It seemed only polite to leave the two women alone to enjoy their intimacy in private. Knowing that neither Freda or Sally were really aware of him anymore, he climbed off the massage table, retrieved his clothes from the floor and dressed hurriedly before letting himself out of the room.

Chapter Six

Shelley had gone off duty by the time Miles got back to the reception desk, and he wasn't sorry. However, this temporary sense of relief was marred somewhat by the appearance of Andrew, who was filling in for a couple of hours.

Miles fidgeted nervously, not sure where to put himself as Andrew slid the registration book across the desk towards him. He found it extremely difficult to look a man directly in the eye only a few minutes after having his cock in his wife's mouth.

'Where's Sally?' Andrew asked, casually enough. 'Did she finish showing you around?'

Miles coughed awkwardly. 'Oh, yes, thanks,' he managed to stammer out. 'But I think she had some business to discuss with the masseuse.'

Because he was studiously trying not to look at Andrew's face, Miles missed the rather pleased little smirk which crossed the man's lips. Business with Freda could only mean one thing, Andrew knew from experience – and it also meant that he was in for a treat later on that evening. After her little sessions with the Swedish girl, Sally always returned as randy as a rattlesnake, and lusting after a hot time between the sheets.

'Just the one night?' he enquired politely, pulling a straight face again.

Miles nodded, trying to avoid conversation and wishing that the man would just let him sign the book and get away again. It was not to be.

'Perhaps you'd like to come into the bar in a few minutes,' Andrew suggested. 'Then we can have that little chat I mentioned earlier.'

Miles racked his brains trying to think of a suitable excuse. He looked awkward and embarrassed, and considerably ill at ease. Suddenly, Andrew felt quite sorry for him. Fully aware of what had been going on, he could understand what Miles was going through. He was, after all, a complete stranger and totally ignorant of what passed for normal day-to-day behaviour in the Paradise Club. Having been frogmarched off and seduced by the manager's wife only moments after walking through the front door, the poor chap must be thinking he had strayed into a nuthouse.

'Look, whatever went on between you and my wife, it's all right,' Andrew said easily. 'We don't have any secrets from each other.'

The straight approach took Miles by surprise. Flustered, he tried to bluff it out. Turning a bright shade of pink, he managed to blurt out: 'Sorry, but I don't know what you're talking about.'

Andrew shrugged. 'Please yourself, but Sally's going to tell me all about it later anyway, and I thought it would make you feel better to bring it out in the open.'

Miles gaped. 'She *tells* you about it?' he asked, still not making a direct admission.

Andrew nodded. 'Sure, that's part of the fun. Mind you, most times I watch anyway.'

'And you don't mind?' Miles wanted to know.

Andrew shrugged again. 'I'd mind a lot more if you were feeling sorry for me as some sort of naive and stupid cuckolded husband,' he pointed out. 'Besides, I get more than my fair share on the side as well, you know. The arrangement works both ways.'

It all made a strange, if somewhat warped, kind of sense, Miles realised. He also had to admit to himself that he was feeling a lot better and more relaxed. He finished signing the registration book and accepted the key which Andrew handed to him. 'Perhaps I might take you up on that drink now,' he said, slipping the key in his pocket.

Minutes later they sat in the almost deserted bar, over a couple of beers.

'So, tell me more about this feature you're planning to shoot,' Andrew suggested, starting the conversation.

Miles was immediately wary. 'Well, actually, it's still very tentative at this stage,' he muttered non-committally. 'This call was intended to be very much a sounding-out operation, if you know what I mean. Sort of a feasibility study if you like.'

He had been hoping to flannel Andrew with a lot of business jargon, but the ploy failed completely. Andrew's eyes narrowed as he shook his head slowly from side to side.

'Well I can't speak for Amanda, of course – but I'm not sure I like the sound of it.'

Miles was puzzled. He couldn't quite understand the man's objection, unless it was something personal. Whatever the reason, it was a hurdle he was going to have to overcome, as Amanda Redfern was bound to at least consider her partner's feelings. Perhaps the direct man-to-man approach was best, he thought. Andrew seemed to be the sort of man who liked straight talking. 'You don't like me, do you?' Miles asked, challengingly.

Andrew took a long pull at his beer before answering. He appeared to be measuring his words carefully. 'Personal viewpoints have nothing to do with it – although I must admit that I'm not sure I trust you.'

It was out in the open now. Miles faced it head-on. 'So what's the objection?' he wanted to know.

Andrew shrugged. 'It's just that I don't think this place needs any more exposure right now,' he said flatly. 'Making any sort of a film here is bound to attract publicity, and we've had all of that we need recently.' He paused, staring Miles straight in the eyes. 'As I'm pretty sure you're only too well aware,' he added, with emphasis.

There was something in the way Andrew was looking at him which made Miles suddenly see him in a new light. Somehow, he got the impression that Andrew knew exactly what was going on. The man was certainly shrewd, Miles thought to himself, and probably a lot more intelligent than he seemed. For that alone, Miles found himself treating Andrew with the first, grudging feelings of respect.

'Well, that's something we shall all have to discuss and take into account tomorrow,' he muttered, effectively closing the subject for the time being. He reached out for Andrew's almost-empty glass. 'Here, let me buy you another beer.'

Several drinks later, and having shared some of Andrew's hair-raising tales of sexual adventures, the two men had formed a degree of male bonding, if not quite friendship. Miles had also been given a few insights into the nature and the workings of the Paradise Country Club, and from what he had learned, his earlier misgivings that the place might be a little too respectable had been completely swept away.

In fact, it was about as respectable as a Moroccan whore-house, he now knew. A seething hot-bed of lust and passion in which everything went, and frequently did. A veritable den of iniquity in which every conceivable sexual gratifica-tion, deviation or fetish could be catered for, and an atmo-sphere in which even the most sexually inhibited person soon became enthusiastically involved in its orgiastic pleasures.

The filming of a sexually exploitive documentary now not only seemed a simple task, it was almost a cop-out, a tame and wishy-washy compromise which belittled the carnal magnificence of the place. It deserved treatment on a grander scale, Miles thought – a full-blown exposé which would place it right up there with the other great sin-bins of history such as the legendary Hellfire Club.

Once again, Miles found himself day-dreaming about his private ambition to film the ultimate pornographic movie. If ever such an epic was to be made, then surely the Paradise Country Club was the natural place to do it. The concept swum intoxicatingly in his head, along with the alcoholic fumes of the drinks he had consumed, and refused to go away. It was the start of an obsession which would eventually lead him into one of the most bizarre and lurid experiences of his life.

But for now, it was probably time to get an early night, Miles thought. The bar was beginning to fill up as the late evening crowd drifted in, and if Andrew's stories were at all accurate, he was quite likely to get caught up in someone else's orgy if he stayed around. Negotiations with Amanda the following day were quite likely to be delicate, and he would need a clear head.

Making his excuses to Andrew, Miles left the bar and went directly to his room. As usually happened when he had consumed a few drinks, sleep came easily to him. Hardly had the waterbed's heaving settled down to a gentle ripple than he was out cold.

He awoke with a start in the darkness, to the certain knowledge that he was not alone in the room. Reaching out his hand, he snapped on the bedside lamp.

Shelley stood at the foot of his bed, wearing a big smile and nothing else. A large bunch of keys dangled from her fingers.

'Hi,' she said, brightly. 'Andrew told me you came up to your room on your own, so I thought you might be able to use a bit of company. I used the pass keys from reception to let myself in.'

Without waiting for a response, the girl sucked in her belly and thrust her chest out, striking a provocative pose. Cupping her hands under her full melon-shaped breasts, she lifted them up to display her pert little coral-tipped nipples to the best advantage. 'Well, what do you think? Good girlie-film material?'

Fully awake now, Miles sat up in bed, propping himself up against the pillows and giving Shelley his full attention. It would have been hard not to do so, for completely naked, with the curves of her lush body accentuated by the yellow-ish light of the single lamp, the girl was a feast for male eyes. Despite the earlier effects of the booze, Miles felt his prick twitch as he began imagining the sensual delights that such a body might deliver.

Only one little worry tugged at the back of his mind, niggling him. Miles regarded Shelley warily as it came to him.

'What makes you think I make girlie films?' he asked cautiously. Shelley giggled, her beautiful tits quivering deliciously. 'Well you do, don't you?' she challenged. 'I thought the name Milestone Films was familiar when you first said it. It was only later that I remembered.'

'Remembered?' Miles queried cautiously.

Shelley nodded. 'I have a male friend who's into that sort of stuff,' she told him. 'He likes showing them on the bedroom ceiling when he's making love. That reminded me of where I'd seen the name Milestone Films before. *Bedtime With Barbara*, for instance – or how about *The Sins of Sexy Sarah*? Ring any bells?'

Caught out, Miles could only look sheepish, but he was still extremely cautious. 'Have you told this to anyone else? Andrew for instance?'

Shelley had a scheming glint in her eye as she answered, suspecting that she had stumbled upon a good thing. 'Why, would you rather I didn't?' she asked, with apparent innocence.

Both her expression and intonation were deliberately challenging, and Miles knew it. He had little choice but to answer honestly. 'Yes, I would, as it happens.'

Shelley giggled again. 'Then I'll be a good girl and keep my mouth shut, if it's doing you a favour. You might want to do me one in return.'

Miles said nothing, but his silence sealed the unspoken

contract between them. Shelley had him temporarily over a barrel and they both knew it. He had no choice now but to keep her sweet, in whatever way she chose.

Shelley was equally aware of this fact, but no longer sure exactly what she wanted from Miles now that she had achieved her primary objective. She had come to his room quite prepared to use her body to put him in her debt. Now, it seemed, that course of action was no longer strictly necessary – although it might be rather a waste to just go away and leave it at that. She could not help noticing the rather obvious bulge beneath the thin duvet cover where Miles' cock had sprung into throbbing hardness. It looked rather promising, she thought.

'You like what you see, obviously,' she murmured sexily, nodding her head towards the spot. 'Now how about you showing me what you've got to offer?'

The girl couldn't be more direct, Miles thought. She was obviously his for the taking, if he wanted her. He wrestled with a minor dilemma for a couple of seconds, his mind saying no but his cock screaming out a most definite yes. However, it was something other than sheer lust which tipped the final balance. If ever he got round to making his great porno movie, he would not have to look much further to find his ideal leading lady, for Shelley positively oozed that rare degree of raw sex appeal which would transfer to film and still smoulder off the screen. It might be interesting to take this opportunity of finding out just how far she was prepared to go, he thought.

He made his mind up on impulse, throwing caution to the winds in much the same way that he threw back the bed cover. Freed from the weight of the duvet, his proud cock jumped up into quivering stiffness.

'Very nice,' Shelley murmured, as much reflecting her own thoughts as handing out a compliment. With a purposeful glint in her eyes, she sauntered over and sat herself down on the side of the bed to examine the meaty treat in more detail.

Having stared at Miles' prick intently for several more seconds, she finally gave a little nod of approval, licking her lips with appreciation. 'Yes, very nice indeed,' she confirmed, reaching out to wrap her slender fingers round its fat stalk. She squeezed it firmly, testing its hardness. The sexy leer flitting across her pretty face showed that Miles had passed the touch, as well as the sight test.

Shelley turned her attention to his balls, sliding her hand under his crotch and weighing them in the palm of her hand. She rolled the swollen globes gently together, making his prick dance in attendance. One slender, tapering finger slipped under his scrotum. Using the very tip of her long and perfectly-manicured fingernail, Shelley lightly scratched the tender puckered flesh around his arsehole. In reflex, Miles' balls jumped in the palm of her hand, his cock swelling even more as his blood began to race.

Miles was in no doubt any longer that he wanted her as much as he had ever wanted any woman. He reached up, slipping his arm around her swan-like neck and pulling her down until she was lying on the bed beside him. Turning onto his side, he threw one leg across her slim waist and pulled himself up on top of her, straddling her stomach. Raising himself on his knees, he gazed down upon her gorgeous body and felt a little vein pulsing in the side of his neck.

His rampant cock reared over the bulging curves of her gorgeous breasts. Reaching down, Miles ran the flat of his hands over their swelling softness, his fingers tracing out their shape and contours, brushing over the small but stiff buds of her nipples. Shelley let out a low, shuddering gasp, her body writhing beneath him as a minor spasm of pleasure rippled through her.

Never slow to miss a cue, Miles devoted more attention to her delightful nipples, now that he had learned how sensitive they were. Pinching each firm fruit between his thumb and forefinger, he tweaked them gently then rolled them around with the balls of his thumbs before pressing them gently into the soft flesh of her breasts.

Shelley moaned softly, her eyes rolling in the throes of rising passion. Looking up, Miles' angry cock jutted stiffly forward in an almost threatening posture, only inches from where his firm hands continued to work her breasts.

A lascivious smile crept across her face. 'Fuck them, Miles,' she breathed huskily. 'Fuck my soft tits with your wonderful hard cock.'

It was not an invitation to resist – particularly when Miles had already fantasised about that very move. He had been wondering what it would feel like to bury the heat of his throbbing hardness in all that soft and cool-looking flesh, lay the full length of his cock along the deep valley of her cleavage.

Leaning forwards, he shuffled his knees until his prick sank down between Shelley's breasts. Squeezing the two creamy mounds together with his hands, Miles wrapped them around the sides of his stiff shaft, burying it in silky softness. He began a slow and gentle rocking motion with his knees, making his prick slide up and down between her tits and feeling his balls bounce sensuously against her breastbone.

For Miles, the physical sensation was a highly erotic experience in itself. For Shelley, part of the sexual kick was purely visual, adding to the overall thrill. Looking down, her mouth drooped open, dribbling saliva at the sight of Miles' prick sliding between her tits. The swollen purplish head popping in and out from the mounds of pale flesh had a highly suggestive quality, and made little shivers ripple down her spine.

Seeing her wet, open mouth, Miles thrust harder, sliding his body up her belly until the head of his cock was only centimetres from her tempting red lips. Shelley responded to the openly suggestive move by extending her tongue and lapping the shiny dome each time it glided within reach.

Miles was sorely tempted to push things to their logical conclusion, stuffing his cock deep into Shelley's enticing looking mouth. Then, remembering his earlier encounter with Sally, he decided against it, aware that oral sex was his one great weakness. Having already had one unbelievable blow-job earlier in the day, it seemed somewhat indulgent. Besides, he did not really want to waste his raging erection in Shelley's mouth, being eager to explore the promise of her lithe and beautiful young body. Past experience had taught him that women with Shelley's type of figure invariably had tight, deep cunts which gripped at a man's cock, encasing it in a succulent tunnel of quivering sensation.

However, Shelley had other ideas for the moment. Her senses inflamed by the sight of Miles' swollen knob so close to her mouth, she craned her head forward, gripping it lightly with her lips. Having thus trapped it, she continued to caress it with her tongue, rolling it around the dome-shaped head and licking delicately at the tiny slit in the top.

Once again, Miles had to fight the urge to fuck her delicious mouth wholeheartedly, enticing though that prospect was. He held back, allowing Shelley to take a few moments of her own pleasure without taking an active part in the act himself.

The head of his cock was no longer enough for her. Shelley thrust her head forward again, her teeth scraping gently against the taut flesh as she sought out the six or seven inches of hot cock still to be enjoyed. Swallowing as much as she could without choking, she sucked it with relish before pulling back and allowing her lips to slide wetly back up the throbbing shaft. Finally, she let his cock pop out of her mouth, sensing that his heart wasn't really in it. She grinned up at him.

'Well, that was pretty good for starters. What do we do now?'

Miles sat up, sliding himself back down her belly until he straddled her thighs. His prick reared up, red and angry-looking with the raging blood which filled it.

'Well I guess I'm as ready as I'll ever be,' he muttered with a faint grin on his face. 'How about you?'

To answer his own question, Miles reached behind his back and felt between Shelley's thighs, probing up towards the soft bush of her pubis and finally slipping three bunched fingers into the moist entrance to her slit. With a slight drilling motion, he pushed them past her quivering little clitoris and deep into her hot and juicy hole.

Shelley's body writhed sensuously. She grunted with pleasure as Miles continued to twist his fingers around inside her, sliding them in and out at the same time to heighten the feeling of penetration. Finally, Miles pulled his fingers out and held them out in front of him, looking at the way they were wet and sticky with love-juice with obvious satisfaction.

'And I guess that says you're ready too,' he observed, knowing that the girl's cunt was now hungry for the entry of a good hard cock. Sliding down between her legs, he reached for his prick and took the shaft in a firm grip, guiding it towards the portals of pleasure.

Shelley's gut tightened in anticipation. Spreading her legs and bringing up her knees slightly, she prepared herself for the beautiful moment of entry. It was not long in coming. With a growing sense of urgency now, Miles waggled the head of his cock between the soft folds of her labia, sliding it up and down against the slippery inner lips.

Shelley let out a long, soulful groan. 'Oh yes, Miles – shove it in. Stick it into me. Ram that big beautiful cock into my cunt as deep as it will go.'

Miles needed no further bidding. With a loud grunt, he thrust forward and plunged into her. His thick cock slid into Shelley's enticing sheath as smoothly as a hot knife into butter. Buried up to his balls, he lay still against her stomach for a while, just savouring the final submission of her gorgeous body beneath his.

It was a moment of almost delirious satisfaction, for the girl delivered every ounce of pleasure that she had promised. Just as Miles had supposed, the inside of her cunt was a tight, hot tunnel of love, sucking and kissing his tumescent flesh like a hundred little caressing mouths. Her compliant body was a firm yet soft cushion beneath his dominance, striking a perfectly matching counterpart. Yin and Yang, male and female, cock and cunt – the hard absorbed by the soft. Shelley's beautiful body seemed to symbolise everything that sex was about, the true magical splendour of man and woman in the ultimate expression of purpose. For surely that *was* the purpose of a woman, Miles thought idly – to take a man's hardness into herself and make it soft again.

He was getting almost mystical, Miles realised suddenly, snapping out of his reverie and concentrating on the matter in hand. Shelley's body squirming beneath his told him that she, at least, had no such esoteric notions of what sex was about. For her, it was purely physical, the simple gratification of the body, not the senses. It was about time he did something about it, Miles decided.

Pulling himself back until the blunt tip of his prick gently pressed against her clitoris, Miles held himself for a split second before ramming back, thrusting his stiff cock back up that wet and wonderful shaft all the way to the neck of her womb.

Shelley gave a thin squeal of delight as the hard meat filled her aching hole. She pulled in her stomach muscles, contracting the walls of her cunt around Miles' intruding prick and sucking it into herself. Flexing and unflexing those same muscles, she was able to massage the sides of the thick shaft as it throbbed inside her.

Miles had already forgotten those few brief moments of sexual philosophising. The exquisite sensations which Shelley was producing in his cock vibrated all the way to his balls, driving him towards a lustful frenzy. Pumping his buttocks, he began to give the girl what she obviously wanted, ramming his stiff cock up and down inside her smooth cunt walls like a steam piston. Her eyes rolling wildly, Shelley ground her hips against his, thrusting her pelvis up against each downward stroke, gasping with pleasure each time her hungry hole swallowed the full length of his prick again. She plunged her body against his, lifting herself on her elbows and rolling her delicious arse from side to side. Her legs came up over his heaving buttocks, her ankles crossing together in the small of his back and locking into a tight vice. Pulling him against her, and throwing herself towards him at the same time, Shelley fucked with all her energy, as though she would never have a cock inside her again. She was gasping for air with every crash of his hips into her soft belly, and making a series of increasingly wild yelps and groans. It was obvious that she had worked herself into a total sexual frenzy, and she showed no signs of slowing down.

Far from worrying about his own possible shortcomings, Miles was now seriously considering the possibility that Shelley would explode into orgasm without him and be too exhausted to help him achieve his own release.

He made an effort to control the speed and the force of his own thrusts, adjusting his rhythm to a slow, regular pumping action and hoping that the girl would follow suit. It did not work. Screaming frantically, Shelley compensated for the change of pace by bucking her hips with a burst of renewed energy, raking her sharp fingernails up and down his naked back as if in frustration.

Miles went back to long, deep strokes, pulling the head of

his prick back until it almost popped out of her soft pussy lips then shoving it in as far as her cervix. Shelley seemed to relax somewhat, her wild screams subsiding to low moans of contentment and her tight cunt opening and closing around the shaft of his cock like a soft, clenching fist.

Suddenly, her body seemed to go into some sort of muscular spasm. She tensed, the softness of her belly becoming a tight knot of bunched tendons. Her legs tightened around his back, and the low moans turned into a throbbing humming sound torn from deep in her throat.

It was now or never, Miles felt. He resumed slamming into her cunt with all his strength, speeding up his pace until his arse was moving in a blur. The humming sound rose in pitch until it was a wail, and finally a long, sustained scream. Shelley's cunt tightened around his cock one last time and went suddenly slack. The scream ended on a note of triumph as she came like a bursting star, her hot juices spraying up between Miles' thighs.

Miles was still thrusting away madly, hardly aware of the girl's orgasm above his own desperate need. Then, suddenly, he felt her legs clenching and unclenching against his back, the wild trembling of her body and the waves of liquid heat pulsing out of her cunt against his prick and balls. The tension evaporated away out of the girl's body, and she seemed to melt into softness.

In that moment of final submission, Miles re-discovered the male/female thing again, the essential essence of sexuality. The girl beneath him was empty now, drained. He was suddenly a man again, filling her with the spurting gift of his seed.

Then there was only the rasping sound of their joint breathing, Shelley's shuddering gasps of pleasure in his ears, and the boiling cauldron of her cunt settling down to a gentle, bubbling simmer.

There was no need for words. They each knew how much pleasure they had each received – and given. Miles rolled off Shelley's sweat-soaked belly, lying flat on his back and staring up at the ceiling. For her part, Shelley curled into an almost foetal position at his side, her blonde head resting lightly upon his chest.

Slowly, the waterbed absorbed the last movements of their violent love-making and began flattening waves into ripples, finally quelling them utterly into stillness. Miles closed his eyes, letting himself sink back into a delicious heaviness which was stealing over his entire body. He felt as though he could happily sleep for a week, or even die and pass into oblivion at that precise moment.

It was only an unknown time later, when Shelley stirred beside him, that he realised he would not sleep much that night. Almost as if in a dream, Miles became aware of her hand creeping up over his thigh and seeking out the warm softness of his flaccid dick and his stomach quivered at her touch.

He turned towards her, pressing his face into her gorgeous tits and sucking the smell of her body into his lungs. He knew then that they would fuck again, and maybe not for the last time.

Chapter Seven

It had been a good day, Amanda congratulated herself, relaxing over her fourth vodka and tonic of the evening in the bar of London's Westchester Hotel. At one stroke she had managed to allay Andrew's worries by getting the media bloodhounds off their backs, and at the same time get a cast-iron promise that the Paradise Club would be left alone in the future.

And it had all been so easy! Using an old, but still effective little trick which has been the salvation of countless corrupt politicians, perverted public figures and embattled businessmen, she had used the power of the gutter press to gag itself.

The technique was essentially simple, but virtually foolproof. It was like finding oneself in a tank full of vicious piranha fish and knowing that a single bite from each would be enough to kill you. So one chose the biggest fish in the tank, or at least the one with the sharpest teeth, and made friends with it. Then it ate up all the other fish out of gratitude.

Applied to the media, the process was much the same. Individually, the press paparazzi and newshound sharks were an undisciplined mob which could tear a victim to pieces. But blood-hungry as they were, virtually all members of the press adhered to their own strange code of ethics and self-regulation. And one of the strongest and fundamental rules of that code was the absolute sanctity of an exclusive story.

So, in Amanda's case, she had simply picked out the most powerful of the daily tabloids, and offered them exclusive rights to the inside story of the Paradise Club scandal in return for them warning everyone else off. The deal made, it had then been merely a question of feeding them a few titillating tit-bits of truth, padded out with a lot of lurid and sensationalist bullshit. The club got a blaze of publicity for one single day, the story would be totally forgotten by the next – and peace would forever after reign.

The bonus, of course, was that the paper had paid handsomely for the story rights, and Amanda was now a cool £25,000 better off, so it was little wonder that she was feeling extremely pleased with herself. The vodkas, on top of the wine she had consumed over a sumptuous lunch at the paper's expense, had topped that feeling of self-satisfaction up so that she was now positively glowing. She felt more secure now than she had in many years. The club was doing well, she had money in the bank, and her personal life was free of any complications. She was a successful young businesswoman, and she had no worries at all.

'Do you mind if I sit here?' a somewhat timid voice enquired at her side, breaking through Amanda's self-congratulatory reverie.

Without waiting for an answer, a man began to clamber up on the bar stool next to her.

Amanda glanced sideways, more out of curiosity than

interest. Her new companion hardly merited either. Amanda saw only a small, rather nondescript little man in his mid-forties who would be just a face lost in the crowd amongst only two other people. Satisfied that he offered neither a threat nor a promise, Amanda ignored him and returned her attention to her drink, finishing it in a single gulp.

'Can I buy you another?' came the polite, but rather nervous enquiry.

Amanda considered the offer for a moment. The man was obviously trying to chat her up, but he seemed harmless enough. He looked out of his depth somehow, as though he didn't quite belong. And he was probably lonely, Amanda thought. His next words confirmed this assessment.

'My name's John Richards – I'm a salesman, from Devon. I'm just up here in London for a couple of days.'

Amanda took pity on him. He was just a simple soul, up from the country in the big city. She feigned a smile. 'How interesting.'

'I travel in ladies' brassieres,' John volunteered.

Amanda repressed a smile, but was unable to resist a joke. 'Must be bloody uncomfortable when you're driving. Not that I'd know – I never wear the things myself.'

John flushed and looked embarrassed. Amanda felt rather guilty for taking the mickey. 'Look, John – I'd love another drink,' she said, trying to make it up to him.

His face brightened up. Summoning the barman over with an extremely awkward and self-conscious wave, he ordered a vodka and tonic for Amanda and a double Scotch for himself. He downed the whisky with a single gulp and immediately ordered another. The sudden intake of alcohol seemed to give him a boost of Dutch courage.

'This is the first time I've done anything like this,' he confided suddenly, with a slightly excited look on his face.

'What, come up to London?' Amanda enquired innocently.

John took another deep swig of his second whisky and flashed her an outrageous wink. 'No – you know – approached one of you girls. It's a lot easier than I thought.'

There seemed to be some special significance in his words, Amanda thought, but she was just that little bit too sozzled to put her finger on it, so she let it pass.

'Staying here, at the Westchester are you?' she asked, trying to make some sort of conversation as payment for the drink.

John looked shocked. 'Good Lord no. I couldn't afford a place like this. I just came in for . . . well, you know.'

Amanda didn't know. She stared at the man blankly.

'Someone I know – a customer of mine – told me this was a good place for it,' John went on. 'And it looks as though he was right.'

Amanda was becoming slightly confused. The fifth vodka and tonic was taking its toll. 'And what else did this friend of yours tell you?' she asked, anxious to steer the conversation back to something she could understand.

John immediately became awkward, even slightly shifty, again. 'He said the going rate was about £100, but I haven't really got that much. I was rather hoping for something around fifty quid.'

It all started falling into place. Suddenly, the penny dropped, and Amanda understood John's reference to 'you girls', and his reason for coming in to the hotel bar. Like many a country bumpkin before him, he was obviously under the impression that the big city was a seething hotbed of vice and iniquity. It was the Dick Whittington legend brought up to the twentieth century – only now the streets of London were supposed to be paved with whores with hearts of gold.

'So – do we talk business here, or in your room?' John was going on.

Amanda made the final connection. The man had assumed her to be a hotel bar hooker, and was making her a direct proposition. Her initial reaction was one of indignation, but then the irony of the situation struck her. John could not really be blamed for his mistake. An attractive young woman, drinking alone in a hotel bar. Even more funny, Amanda thought, was that only a couple of years ago, he wouldn't have been far wrong. In her escort agency days, before she had inherited the Paradise Club from a grateful client, Amanda had frequently picked up her dates in the bars of London hotels.

She looked John over again, seeing him in a new light. He wasn't so different to any one of them, she realised. Certainly far from good-looking, but not ugly. Amanda had always drawn the line at really repulsive men, or those who looked or acted at all suspect. John was just *ordinary*. A real John, in fact, Amanda thought, smiling inwardly.

Remembering those old days, a buzz of devilment ran through her. Just suppose, she thought. Just suppose she played the game through, just for the hell of it? What did she really have to lose? She was stuck in the Westchester Hotel, having had far too many drinks to drive back to the club safely, and she was getting bored. One glance around the bar was enough to confirm there was little chance of excitement. Being alone in the city gave her a kind of anonymity. Nobody knew her, and she would probably never bump into John again in her life. Anything she did tonight would be outside real time, almost outside reality itself. As though it never happened at all.

Strangely, just thinking about it gave her an odd thrill, appealing to her sense of the perverse. To act, for one night, as a prostitute with a complete stranger was outrageous – but it was also an adventure. Besides, she was feeling particularly magnanimous towards the world, and she had the chance to make a lonely man happy, if only for a few hours.

Amanda made up her mind on impulse. She flashed John one of her most devastating smiles, laying her hand over his in a suggestive promise. 'Don't worry about the money now, John,' she purred. 'Let's just have another couple of drinks and get to know each other better.'

It seemed like a good idea that John wasn't going to argue with. He downed the rest of his double Scotch and ordered another round.

'So, are you married, John?' Amanda asked, conversationally.

John shook his head woefully.

'Girlfriend?'

John gulped down his second drink, staring fixedly at the half-empty glass. 'I have a bit of a problem with women,' he said, miserably.

Amanda managed to make herself look sympathetic, even though she suspected that she'd heard the story before. 'Shy?' she asked.

John shook his head again. 'It's more of a physical thing,' he admitted. He fell silent for a long while, looking embarrassed and troubled.

He obviously had something he wanted to say, Amanda thought, but was having trouble opening up to a stranger. She patted his hand again. 'Come on, you can tell me,' she urged.

John drained the last of his drink and quickly ordered another, downing it in a single gulp. His eyes looked slightly blurred as he turned back towards Amanda in conspiratorial fashion. 'Actually, it's to do with my sexual equipment,' he confessed finally. 'The size of it – you know what I mean?'

Amanda nodded her head understandingly. Now she was absolutely sure she'd heard the story before, but she seemed to have cast herself in the role of confessor and she had little choice but to play it through. 'Too small, huh?' she murmured sympathetically.

John regarded her with a look of abject misery. 'I could probably learn to cope with that,' he said dejectedly. 'My problem is that women say it's too big. It frightens them off.'

Amanda did a quick double-take. Either John was throwing her the most original line she'd heard in years, or he was on the up and up. It sounded interesting. She stared him directly in the eye, searching for the slightest trace of guile. He continued to look miserable.

'Let's get this straight. You're telling me that you're packing oversized equipment and women *complain* about it?'

John nodded. 'I guess they think I'm some kind of freak, and it scares them.'

Amanda was pretty sure John was telling the truth now,

and she was totally hooked. Mere interest had given way to total fascination. There was the slightest hint of urgency in her tone when she spoke again.

'Look, John – suppose we skip the drinks and getting to know each other bit and go up to my room right now?' she suggested.

John shrugged. 'Suits me. Maybe room service could send up a bottle of Scotch or something. When I've had a few it doesn't get quite so hard.'

He was just raising his glass to his lips again as he delivered this piece of information. None too discreetly, Amanda's hand shot out, gripping his wrist and restraining him. 'Let's think about the Scotch later on,' she murmured, making sure that he put his glass back down on the counter. She slipped off her stool, pulling him away from the bar. Keeping a tight grip on his wrist, she began to lead him towards the nearest lift.

Amanda's room was on the third floor. She dragged John out of the lift and down the corridor, opening the door and ushering him inside. Closing the door and locking it, Amanda strolled over to the bed and sat down expectantly. She waited for several moments as John stood awkwardly in the middle of the room, shuffling his feet nervously.

'Well, aren't you going to take your clothes off?' Amanda asked him at last.

John grinned at her sheepishly. 'Oh, that's the form, is it?' he muttered uncertainly. 'I wasn't sure if you girls had some sort of routine or something.' Still looking embarrassed, he began to undress, folding his clothes neatly as he peeled them off and draping them across the back of the bedside chair.

Amanda's eyes followed every move like a hawk, glinting slightly with eager anticipation. She paid particular attention as John dropped his trousers, looking out for an especially promising bulge in his underpants. She was somewhat disappointed as his trousers slipped to the floor, revealing a pair of loose and baggy boxer shorts which gave very little away.

Seconds later, however, it was time for these too to be shed, and Amanda licked her lips as the moment of truth approached.

Perhaps he had been shooting her a line after all, Amanda thought, as John's flaccid prick and balls sprang into view. Seen from a distance of six or seven feet, his sporting set did not look particularly impressive, let alone something to send women screaming off in terror. Feeling slightly miffed, Amanda uncoiled from the bed and sauntered over for a closer inspection.

She had expected to see something resembling a horse's appendage dangling down to the region of his kneecaps, but there was virtually no dangle at all. Indeed, apart from its thickness, if there was anything unusual about John's cock at all, it was its remarkably dormant appearance and strange shape. Instead of hanging down, it appeared to grow out at an odd sideways angle from his dangling balls, then curl itself around in a ball like a soft toy or a sleeping kitten. Had it not been for the pale colour, it would have reminded Amanda very much of a black pudding in a butcher-shop cold cabinet.

Feeling distinctly cheated, Amanda's lips curled into a rather scornful sneer.

'And that's it, is it?' she asked, frowning.

John nodded his head. 'It's not so bad when it's like this,' he muttered apologetically. 'It's when it gets hard it's a bit threatening.'

Amanda found it extremely difficult to imagine that any woman would find the soft coil of flesh anything but mildly amusing. Far from offering any threat, it looked as though it was crying out to be cuddled or squeezed. She continued to stare at it doubtfully, growing more certain by the second that John's cock was completely harmless. There was not the slightest twitch or sign of movement. To all outward appearances, the thing appeared to be dead.

'How many Scotches did you have before I met you?' Amanda enquired rather pointedly.

John looked down shamefacedly, shaking his head. 'I don't think it's brewer's droop,' he protested weakly. 'I think it might be because I'm a bit inhibited. I've never done anything like this before.'

Amanda was not convinced. John started to fidget nervously as her expression became increasingly grim.

'Look, it's just that this is all a bit cold-blooded,' he stammered out finally. 'Perhaps if you showed me your breasts, or something like that.'

Amanda thought about that one. She was rapidly getting the impression that she had somehow been set up, that she was being taken for a ride. Yet beneath this still lurked the faintest niggling doubts. Her curiosity had been whetted by John's story of his monster cock, and she would not be really satisfied until it was proven or disproven. Finally, with a resigned shrug, she started to unpick the buttons of her blouse.

John's eyes widened as Amanda slipped the blouse off

over her shoulders and allowed her lush, coral-tipped breasts to swing free in all their naked glory. As she had so truthfully told him earlier, Amanda never wore a bra, being one of the few lucky women whose breasts were firm and shapely enough to need no artificial support. John feasted his eyes on the twin mounds of mammary perfection for some time before tearing them away to glance down hopefully at his prick.

There was little change. Sighing deeply, John looked at Amanda again, sheepishly.

'It always takes a bit of time to get going,' he muttered defensively. 'I think it's something to do with the sheer amount of blood it needs to pump it up.'

Amanda wasn't really listening. She was now increasingly sure that the true nature of John's problem was not oversized equipment at all but simple old-fashioned impotence. It looked as though she had been conned – and she wasn't very pleased about it.

Her annoyance showed on her face, and John could read it. With a mounting sense of desperation, he realised that time was running out fast. This knowledge lent him a false sense of bravado, overcoming his natural shyness.

'Look, perhaps if you just played with it a little bit,' he blurted out, more in hope than expectation. 'I'm sure that will do the trick.'

Amanda glared at him, her rising anger softened slightly by the look of desperate sincerity on the man's face. Despite everything, he still seemed so damned convincing, she thought. She sighed deeply, realising that she didn't really have anything to lose by humouring him for a few more moments.

She moved towards him, reaching down between his legs rather self-consciously. Grasping the curled-up sausage, she weighed it in her palm, squeezing its rubbery softness with her fingers and pulling it gently towards her.

Straightened out, John's cock did start to look more generously proportioned, although still far short of being truly impressive. Amanda's fingers stroked along its under-side, feeling for the tell-tale pulsing vein which might betray signs of life. Other than a faint and sluggish throb, there was nothing.

'Do you mind if I stroke your breasts?' John asked politely.

Amanda shrugged her aquiescence with casual disdain. Having come this far, there didn't seem much point in getting uptight about letting the man cop a quick feel.

'Help yourself,' she muttered generously, slipping her fingers under his balls and beginning to tickle them.

John accepted the offer eagerly, reaching up to wrap his hands squarely over Amanda's firm tits. Letting the nipples nestle into the gaps between his fingers, he began to knead the soft flesh crudely, like a baker pummelling mounds of dough.

At least one thing he had told her was most certainly true, Amanda realised. John had obviously had extremely limited experience when it came to women. She had come across more sophisticated fondling techniques behind the bicycle sheds back in her secondary school days. However, what John lacked in finesse, he made up for in enthusiasm. His fingers flew over her breasts, pinching and squeezing them unmercifully.

Tickling his balls seemed to be evoking some kind of a

response, Amanda thought, feeling a growing warmth from the soft flesh lying across her wrist. She grasped the floppy shaft again, pulling and squeezing it gently.

John let out a little whoop of delight. 'Ooh – I think that's doing it,' he announced happily, redoubling his efforts to mash Amanda's tits into lumps of jelly.

Amanda glanced down at the spongy organ in her hand, noting that it was indeed now showing distinct signs of waking up. With a series of convulsive little twitches, it was now beginning to straighten out of its own accord, and there were definite signs of swelling in both length and thickness.

Amanda fingered the underside again, and was gratified to feel that the dull throb she had identified earlier was now a powerful and regular pulse. She continued to squeeze the stiffening organ, becoming increasingly more enthusiastic about her task as it began to grow . . . and grow . . . and grow.

It seemed that her manual ministrations were no longer strictly necessary. Once set off, John's cock had developed a life of its own, and was awakening with a vengeance. Amanda stepped back to admire the results of her handiwork as the sleeping giant arose to full, throbbing erection. She watched, fascinated, as the huge domed head crept up John's stomach towards his belly button and continued to swell beyond it. Finally, with a series of little convulsions, the mighty weapon jerked into complete stiffness and stopped growing.

Amanda's eyes popped as she realised that John had been telling the truth all along. His cock was, without a shadow of doubt, the most amazing piece of male equipment that she had ever seen. A good eight inches long and now as straight and stiff as a pikeshaft, it reared up from John's groin, pressed flatly against his belly with the huge swollen helmet resting just under the bottom of his ribcage. Besides its formidable length, it was also immensely thick and fat. Amanda estimated that the base of its shaft was probably around the circumference of her own wrist, and although it tapered slightly towards the head, it was little wonder that the super-weapon caused some women to shy away in fear. Thickly veined and knobbly, John's huge cock had a particularly angry and menacing appearance, as though it was a weapon of torture rather than pleasure.

Filled with a slightly morbid fascination rather than excitement, Amanda could not just look at the stiff monster without feeling it again, now that it was fully erect. Like an animal mesmerised by a snake, she moved forward again and reached for it, wrapping her slim fingers around the massive shaft almost nervously.

Her first touch was enough to confirm that the oversized joypole differed in one other respect from most cocks she had encountered. In Amanda's considerable experience, even the hottest and hardest of pricks retained a degree of resilience, of fleshy muscularity. John's solid-looking weapon felt rock-hard and unyielding – nearer to solid bone than to flesh. Squeezing the rigid shaft made no impression at all. Flexing her wrist, Amanda tried bending it, but it was as inflexible as a metal rod.

'Well, what do you think?' John asked. 'Do you think you can handle it?'

Amanda slid her fingers up and down the prodigious length of the blood-engorged tool, sensing the sheer size and power of it. She looked up at John with a wry grin on her face. 'Oh, I can *handle* it. I'm just not too sure if I can do anything else with it.'

The hopeful expression on John's face faded, and he looked utterly forlorn again. 'Not you as well,' he muttered miserably. 'I'd really hoped that a girl like you wouldn't find it quite so off-putting.'

Amanda had reached the bulbous head of his cock now, and was squeezing it in her palm. It felt like a cricket ball.

'Perhaps I could just slide it in and out between your thighs,' John suggested. 'It'd be better than nothing, and I'd pay you just the same. Otherwise I'll just have to wank it off. Once it's up like this, you see, it won't go down again.'

That sounded like a terrible waste, Amanda thought. Having got over her initial shock, she had started seriously considering John's cock as a practical proposition. Fondling the throbbing monster in her hand, she was aware of her growing sexual excitement, even if it was tempered with the faintest sense of trepidation. She wondered, breathlessly, what it would feel like to have such a huge rod stretching her pussy lips to their fullest capacity, ramming its way up the tight tunnel of her cunt. Vague memories of adolescent fantasies and fears stirred in the back of her mind. Before her first time, before she had sent her virginity on a strictly one-way ticket to oblivion, there had always been those little nagging doubts, the fears of inexperience. Suspicions that the angry and seemingly huge male pricks she had encountered in petting sessions could not possibly fit inside her, that they would split her in two, or spear into her belly and cause heaven-knows-what kind of internal damage.

She had a similar feeling again. Not quite of danger, not quite of excitement but a mixture of the two, something in between. A sort of delicious dread, a reckless abandon and the wild thrill of the unknown. She still had serious doubts about her ability to take John's mighty cock inside her, but she knew she was going to try her damnedest.

There was a purposeful glint in her eyes as she looked up at John's troubled face. 'Believe me, I'm not going to waste a beautiful cock like this on a wank,' she assured him. 'I'm still not quite sure how we're going to do it – but we're going to do it.'

To back up her words, Amanda quickly stripped off her skirt and panties. Taking John by the hand, she led him across to the bed.

'Lie down on your back,' she commanded him. 'I think the best bet is for me to try to mount you, rather than the other way round.'

His heart surging with expectation, John did as he was told, laying down with his legs tightly together. Stretched out like that, and viewed from above, his massive pole looked even more daunting. Amanda felt a distinct lump rising in her throat as she gazed down upon the meaty weapon. She dropped one hand to the mouth of her cunt, slipping three bunched fingers between its fat lips.

She was already wet with anticipation, Amanda realised gratefully – but was it enough? Something told her she was going to need every fluid ounce of lubricating love-juice her glands could produce to ease the monster prick inside her. Moving her fingers around inside her cunt, Amanda flicked her thumb back and forth across her erect clitoris to stimulate the flow. Only when the excess juice was beginning to dribble down the insides of her thighs did she feel confident enough to proceed further.

Climbing up onto the bed, she threw one leg over John's thighs and rose up onto her knees. John's cock was still lying flat against his belly. Wrapping her palm around the incredibly thick base of its shaft, Amanda pulled it up into an upright position and pressed the swollen head into the moist cleft between her soft labial lips. Rising on her haunches and rocking gently backwards and forwards from the waist, she smeared her own secretions liberally around the top three or four inches of his cock.

Satisfied that it was now slick and shiny with lubricant, Amanda spread her legs, stretching out the mouth of her cunt as wide as possible. Now came the tricky part, she thought.

John's cock danced in her hand as she pulled it gingerly into position, settling the blunt dome between the slippery folds of her fat and swollen cunt lips once again. Delicately, as though directing a precision operation, she adjusted her own position until her knees were spread as far apart as possible and the open and hairy mouth of her wet cunt was poised above the .throbbing head of its prey. Carefully, gingerly, she began to lower herself until she could feel the ball-like tip settle into the hot crevice and push against the faint restriction of her vaginal muscles.

Feeling the head of John's mighty tool knocking on the door to her private entrance, as it were, Amanda experienced a strange change of mood. So far, she had approached the whole operation almost cold-bloodedly, with the clinical detachment of an operation or a medical experiment. Now, sensing the sheer size and repressed masculine power of the great cock about to ram into her, she felt the first stirrings of real lust, a genuine hunger to be filled with such a magnificent organ. She shuddered with anticipatory pleasure as the smooth head popped through her oozing cunt lips, easing its way into the enclosing walls of her tight shaft. Still tempering her growing desire with caution, she wriggled her arse from side to side, bearing down with slowly increasing pressure as the movement eased the first few inches of penetration.

John groaned with ecstasy as he felt the moist heat of Amanda's cunt sucking at the sensitized head of his sadly under-used prick. It was perhaps two full years since he had managed to get it inside a woman, and then only a huge fat slag who had been so blind drunk that she wasn't really aware of what was going on. He could hardly dare to believe that now he was about to be fucked with real enthusiasm by a gorgeous young woman who obviously took pride and pleasure in her job. He felt a strong urge to thrust upwards with a single violent movement, ramming his cock into her juicy cunt once and for all. Wisely, he resisted the impulse, letting Amanda control matters to her own satisfaction. A woman of her considerable experience and expertise would certainly know what she was doing, he felt sure, and he could not afford to lose his chance now that he was this close.

The fat head of John's cock was well into position now, plugging Amanda's hole as tightly and efficiently as a champagne cork. Continuing to gyrate her arse in small circles, she bore down with increasing pressure, feeling the thick shaft creep in inch by precious inch. Her cunt felt stretched to the limit, and although still a little short of

actual pain, the sensation was definitely physically uncomfortable. Amanda wondered, somewhat fancifully, if she was
experiencing something akin to childbirth but in reverse.

She pushed down again, and was disappointed to find that
John's massive prick refused to slide any further up her
ravenous tunnel. With a little sob of frustration, she rolled
her arse wildly, thrusting downwards more forcibly, but it
was no good. The fat column of flesh was stuck like a rat in a
pipe, and all her efforts were in vain.

Amanda felt almost physically sick with frustration. To be
cheated of the full splendour of such a rare and magnificent
prize was like a punishment. Amanda racked her brains,
trying to sort out both the problem and the solution to it.

Basically, it was a question of lubrication, she realised.
The fat head of John's prick was lodged tight inside her cunt,
effectively stopping the full flow of her juices from dribbling
down to wet the thicker part of the shaft. Offhand, she could
only think of pulling herself off and trying again – but then
another idea struck her.

There was more than one way to skin a cat, Amanda
thought to herself – and more than one type of lubricant.
Certain that she had found the solution to her problem, she
pulled her cunt off the head of John's cock with a loud
plopping sound and jumped off the bed, pulling at his arm to
join her.

'It's not going to work like this,' she told him breathlessly.
'Come with me, I've got a better idea.'

Having little choice in the matter, John allowed her to drag
him off the bed and across the bedroom towards the en-suite
shower unit. Jumping into the cubicle, Amanda set the
thermostat control to a gentle warmth and turned on the

water, letting it spray all over her body. Taking down a bottle of shower gel dangling from the curtain rail, she squirted a healthy measure into her palm and then smeared it into her pubic hair, working it up into a rich, creamy lather.

She pulled John into the cubicle behind her, handing him the tube of gel and motioning for him to follow suit. John got the idea quickly. Grinning, he frothed the soapy mixture all around his balls and up the thin hairs on his stomach, making sure that he coated the full length of his cock with a thick layer of slippery suds.

Amanda turned her back on him, spreading her feet the full width of the shower tray and placing the palms of her hands against the plastic side of the cubicle. She thrust out her pert little arse provocatively, leaving John in no doubt as to what to do next.

Sidling up behind her, he took his slippery love-machine in his hand and guided it into place beneath the rounded cheeks of Amanda's arse, the blunt head once more pressed against the soapy lips of her cunt.

Wriggling her pelvis, Amanda backed onto it, feeling a glowing satisfaction as the thick tool now slid into her like a well-greased piston rod. Half-turning her head, she spoke to John over her shoulder.

'You can start pumping now – but not too hard and not too fast.'

John was only too eager to obey. Edging closer to Amanda's delicious rump, he pushed forward with his hips, sending the first five or six inches of his cock smoothly into her wet tunnel. One final, gentle shove, and he was buried in her up to the hilt, his heavy balls dangling between the cheeks of her arse. His hands came up and under her armpits, grasping her ripe breasts.

Amanda let out a long, shuddering sigh of pleasure as the mighty shaft soared into her, all the way to the very mouth of her womb. It was every bit as satisfying as she had fantasised, but more fulfilling than she could ever have imagined. It was not so much like being totally and utterly filled with cock, as being aware of herself as nothing more than one huge cunt. The external parts of her body didn't seem to exist anymore, or if they did, she was strangely cut off from them. Even her brain didn't seem to be functioning normally, registering no thoughts other than the pure sensation of being fucked. She was just a hollow vessel, inside which a huge and powerful cock throbbed and thrusted, pumped and probed every internal inch. As John continued to obey her instructions and thrust his great cock into her with slow, gentle strokes, Amanda gave herself over to a sensation of total bliss in which time itself seemed to have been suspended.

The knowledge that she was going to come surfaced somewhere in the recesses of her mind like an old memory. It was still not a clear thought even as a rippling wave of tingling spasms started up somewhere deep in her belly and began to flow out through the rest of her body. Detached from it all, Amanda heard her own squeals of pleasure only as a disembodied voice, something in the background of a dream. Then, as her body erupted into full orgasm, reality crashed in again in a turbulent mixture of sensations.

Grunts, gasps and blurted out obscenities tumbled from her lips. Amanda's hands pummelled against the plastic wall of the shower cubicle. She rolled her arse furiously, jabbing her buttocks back in feverish, stabbing strokes which impaled her even deeper on John's fleshy spike. Muscles in her belly clenched tightly in a series of involuntary spasms, clamping the wet walls of her cunt around the intruding cock to squeeze it tightly, press and suck out its very juices.

A secondary wave of orgasm followed close on the heels of the first, crashing over her like a breaking wave. John's huge prick was moving in and out of her cunt like a hydraulic pump now, making her juices flow anew. Wet and slippery, it glided smoothly up and down the walls of her love-tunnel with ease now, as though it had been precision-made to fit and making Amanda wonder why she had ever doubted her ability to accommodate it. Yet slick and smooth as its thrusting passage was, the sensation of complete penetration remained. Between gasps for breath, Amanda screamed out for John to give her more of his wonderfully satisfying weapon.

'Come on, really fuck me now,' she urged him. 'Ram it in as hard as you like.'

Feeling her hot juices scalding the sides of his prick, and knowing that he had totally satisfied her, John let himself go and chased his own, increasing urgent needs. Speeding up his tempo, he sent his cock soaring all the way up to the neck of her womb again, his arse moving in a blur as he pumped in short, jabbing strokes which almost lifted Amanda's feet off the floor of the shower.

Amanda squealed with delight at the renewed assault. Sliding her feet together, she clenched her abdominal muscles tightly and thrust her beautiful arse backwards and upwards.

John's balls slapped wetly against her firm cheeks with every savage in-stroke. He was grunting like an animal now with each thrust, partly from exertion and partly from awareness of his own, imminent orgasm. There was a feeling of weakness in his legs, a tingling, fluttering sensation which threatened to paralyse his muscles. His rhythm faltered for a brief moment, his stabbing thrusts becoming erratic and half-hearted. Then he rallied, steeling himself for one last burst. Drawing on deep reserves of energy, he rocked his hips frantically back and forth for another fifteen or twenty seconds and finally jabbed in one last violent thrust that made Amanda's teeth clack together. With a loud bellow of triumph, he pumped his creamy emission deep into her cunt.

Amanda screamed out as she came for the third and final time, her insides seeming to turn into jelly. Totally sated, and totally exhausted, it was all she could do to stay on her feet as John's cock pulsed inside her for nearly a minute before he finally withdrew.

Gasping for breath, they both managed to stagger out of the shower cubicle and back across the room to the bed, where they collapsed.

'I just don't know how to thank you enough,' John said gratefully, when he had at last got his breath back.

Amanda said nothing, but the Cheshire-cat grin on her face spoke volumes.

John sat upright on the bed. 'Now, about the money?' he muttered a little awkwardly. 'Shall I just leave it on the bedside table as I leave?'

Amanda shook her head. 'Forget the money,' she told him. 'This one's on me.'

John looked at her blankly, not understanding.

Amanda grinned at him. 'Let's call it a sales promotion or something,' she suggested. 'You're my hundredth customer tonight, so you get a freebie.'

The joke went over John's head. He continued to stare at her in incomprehension.

Amanda decided to put an end to the little charade. John deserved to know that he had just made love to a woman for pleasure, not for payment. Besides, another little idea had just occurred to her.

'Look, I'm not a hooker,' she told him flatly. 'But you'd obviously made that assumption and I decided to play along with it for a bit of a giggle. As it turned out, the laugh was on me, because you just gave me one of the best tumbles of my life.'

The look of pride and rapturous joy which crossed John's face told Amanda that she had done the right thing. Perhaps now he would not be so self-conscious and negative about his superb cock. Given a bit of confidence, and finding the right women, the man had a pretty good sex life to look forward to.

In fact, that was one little area in which Amanda might be able to help him out a bit. If there was one place where the right women could be found in abundance, it was the Paradise Country Club.

'Look, do you have a business card or something?' she asked him. 'I'd like to be able to get in touch with you.'

John looked bemused, but finally got off the bed and retrieved a small business card from the pocket of his jacket. Amanda took it, placing it carefully on the bedside table.

'Don't be surprised if you find yourself invited down for a weekend in the country in the not too distant future,' she said mysteriously.

Amanda left it at that, not wanting to make any firm promises. But something told her that Freda and Sally would be very interested in the tale of a super-cock salesman, and John could well find himself a frequent visitor to the Paradise Club.

Chapter Eight

As it turned out, Amanda's story of her unexpected sexual adventure was somewhat overshadowed by the presence of Miles Lansing. She hardly had time to unpack her overnight bag before both Sally and Freda had regaled her with glowing reports of the man's sexual equipment and Shelley had broken the news that she was on the verge of becoming a famous film star.

It was not until she talked to Andrew that Amanda was able to get the faintest impression of what the man was actually doing there. He gave her the few facts he had gleaned and let her think about it for a while.

'Well, what do you think?' he asked finally, when Amanda appeared to have mulled it over for long enough.

Amanda shrugged. 'I guess I ought to go and see the man,' she said. 'That's if there's anything left of him after Freda, Sally and Shelley have all had a go.'

Andrew grinned. 'Well he hasn't come out of his room yet this morning, and it's already past eleven-thirty. So either Shelley finished him off, or he's a man who likes a late breakfast.'

'Maybe Shelley *was* his breakfast,' Amanda countered. 'Or from what I hear of her sexual preferences, he was hers.'

Leaving Andrew working that one out, she headed for Miles' room, after first checking the number from the visitor's book.

There was a lot of information to be gained about a man from the way he first looked at you, Amanda had decided long ago. Some men's initial reaction at encountering an attractive woman was to undress them with their eyes, reduce them immediately to little more than objects of pleasure. Others were even more openly lascivious, making a woman feel cheap and unclean. And some, although not many, had the uncanny ability to deliver the greatest possible compliment without even saying a word.

Miles Lansing was one of those rare few, Amanda decided, as he opened the door in response to her knock. He was smiling, even if he looked a trifle weary.

'I'm Amanda Redfern,' Amanda said, getting straight to the point. 'I understand you wanted to see me?'

Miles nodded, pulling open the door in welcome. 'Yes, thanks for coming. Please come in,' he said warmly. He retreated to the window as Amanda entered the room and closed the door behind her.

Miles flashed her an apologetic smile, rubbing at his chin, which was showing a dark stain of stubble.

'I hope you'll forgive my appearance,' he muttered. 'I wasn't expecting you, and I haven't shaved yet.'

Amanda smiled. 'Hard night?' she enquired, with a suggestive edge to her voice.

Miles grinned. 'Yeah – but it wasn't hard for long,' he shot back. 'This is really some place you got here.'

The joke was openly sexual, but delivered with panache. Always a sucker for a man with a sense of humour,

Amanda's first impressions of Miles Lansing were confirmed. She liked him instinctively, even if she didn't actually find him immediately physically attractive. Not that there was anything wrong with the man, he just didn't happen to be the type she usually went for. But he was pleasant, he had a way of making a woman feel good, and she felt relaxed in his company. It was a good start.

'So, what's the deal?' Amanda wanted to know. 'Andrew tells me you want to make some sort of film here.'

Miles was quiet for a while, sizing Amanda up. He was pretty sure that he'd made a good initial impression, but perhaps he ought to soften her up a bit more before he told her too much.

'Well, it's not quite as simple as that,' he said finally. 'Perhaps you could wait until I've had a wash and shave and then we'll go downstairs and discuss things over a cup of coffee?'

It sounded a reasonable idea, and in fact Amanda felt slightly relieved at the suggestion. It had been in the back of her mind that Miles might try on the old seduction routine, which would have been a mistake. She was warming to the man fast, and had no wish to spoil a promising friendship.

'Sure,' she said brightly. 'Why don't I leave you in privacy to do your thing and then you can come down and join me in the breakfast room when you're ready?'

The suggestion seemed to suit them both. Miles escorted Amanda politely to the door and out into the corridor. 'Give me about five minutes,' he said cheerily, and ducked back into the room.

Amanda walked down the hallway towards the stairs, experiencing an odd sense that someone was watching her.

The feeling was confirmed as she reached the head of the staircase, and Shelley pounced out from around the corner.

'Been to see Miles, have you?' the girl asked innocently enough, but Amanda sensed a slight edge behind the words. One glance into Shelley's eyes was enough to tell Amanda what it was. Every woman knew the look of the little green-eyed god called jealousy.

'Relax, Shelley – he's not really my type,' Amanda said, anxious to reassure the girl. They had always had a more than cordial working relationship, and she had no wish to spoil it.

Shelley looked slightly mollified. 'He's nice though – isn't he?' she asked, as if seeking confirmation of her own good taste.

Amanda shrugged. 'I suppose so, if you like that sort of thing,' she conceded. 'But take my word for it – it's strictly business. Mr Lansing wants to use the club to make one of his films.'

If she had promised Shelley the gift of eternal youth and beauty, the girl couldn't have looked more rapturous. If Miles was planning to make a film right here in the club, then her chance of stardom was nearer than she had dared believe. She looked pleadingly at Amanda. 'And you're going to give him permission – aren't you?'

Amanda shook her head vaguely. 'I don't know yet,' she admitted honestly. 'We're going to discuss it over coffee in about five minutes.'

Shelley's eyes glittered with animal cunning. She cast a thoughtful glance in the direction of Miles' bedroom. 'I suppose you couldn't make that about half an hour instead, could you?' she asked. 'I've got a bit of business with Miles myself.'

Amanda got the message and smiled. 'Breakfast time, is it?' she asked, with a hint of friendly sarcasm in her tone.

Shelley flashed her a sexy grin. 'Oh no, we had breakfast,' she said suggestively. 'This is elevenses. Besides, I have a rather interesting piece of news for him.'

Amanda didn't really have to think about it. It didn't really matter to her when she talked to Miles, and Shelley was obviously smitten. 'Half an hour,' she conceded. 'But no longer.'

The girl danced away happily down the corridor towards Miles' room. Smiling to herself, Amanda began to descend the stairs, heading towards the massage and treatment suite. She could use the extra time winding up Freda with the story of John and his giant cock.

Stripped down to his underpants in front of the washroom mirror, Miles was just about to raise his safety razor to his throat as he heard the bedroom door burst open. His first, somewhat fanciful thought was that Amanda had returned, having been totally bowled over by his manly charms. It was a hopeful, but extremely pleasant daydream to have. Miles had been more than impressed by his first sight of the delectable Miss Redfern.

Seeing the advancing figure of Shelley in the mirror came as almost a disappointment. Miles tensed as the girl rushed up behind him, mashing her full breasts into his back and throwing her arms around his hips, where her hands settled possessively over the soft bulge of his prick.

Miles let out a half-hearted groan. 'Dammit, Shelley – I haven't had a chance to shave yet,' he protested.

The girl was not to be put off. 'Don't worry about it,' she

said casually, tossing his objection aside. 'That's not the end of you I'm interested in right now.'

With that she moved her hands to his hips, spinning him round until he was facing her. With no further ado, she dropped to her knees in front of him and pulled his skimpy briefs down to his knees, burying her face in his groin. Seconds later, her hot tongue began slavering over his soft cock and balls.

Miles groaned again – this time a little more forcefully. 'Look, we haven't got time for this. I have to meet Amanda in five minutes, and it's important.'

Shelley left his prick alone for just long enough to look up at him. 'Relax, I just got you a stay of execution,' she informed him. 'We have as much time as this is going to take.'

She renewed her ministrations on his flaccid tool. Gripping the soft skin beneath the circumcised dome gingerly between her teeth like a mother cat picking up a kitten, she began to waggle it gently from side to side, as though to shake it into life. Reaching up between his thighs, she cupped one hand under the soft bag of his scrotum and started to jiggle his balls up and down.

Resigning himself to the inevitable, Miles leaned back against the sink and let himself enjoy this twin assault on his sexual equipment. There was a faint tingling sensation in his groin as his cock began to stir into erection. The soft tool swelled rapidly as the heated blood of passion began to flow into the fleshy tube.

Shelley gurgled with delight. As Miles' cock throbbed gently into semi-hardness, she wrapped her mouth over it, pressing it between her soft red lips and rolling her tongue around its swelling thickness.

Pumping blood had soon completed the miracle of transformation, and Miles' handsome prick jerked into full and
throbbing erection. Shelley could no longer contain the full
length of the generously-endowed tool in her mouth, but
she continued to gobble it greedily, alternately licking the
full length with a hot, wet tongue and sucking on the
swollen head with her pursed lips. Rolling saliva around in
her throat and squirting it to the front of her mouth, she
bobbed her head up and down so that her wet and slippery
lips glided up and down the stiff shaft. Little rivulets of
dribble seeped from the corners of her mouth and ran
messily down her chin, but Shelley was past caring about
table manners.

The whole of her upper body was rocking now as she
thrust her head forward and back, sliding her lips up and
down Miles' rock-hard organ. Miles felt weak at the knees
as Shelley's superb fellatio techniques took him further and
further down the one-way road towards orgasm. He leaned
back harder against the sink, helping to support his own
weight. Looking down, the sight of Shelley's lush lips
moving up and down his stiff cock was another little turn-on
in itself. He shivered with the delicious pleasure of it all,
making little grunting sounds of appreciation in his throat.

Perhaps sensing that she was bringing him on too
quickly, Shelley changed her technique. She let his cock
plop out of her mouth and turned her attention to his
dangling balls, lapping them with slow, deliberate strokes of
her wet tongue. Moving upwards again, she licked along the
throbbing underside of his cock all the way to the top,
finishing the manoeuvre off by planting an almost chaste
little kiss on the smooth head.

Miles felt his cock dance in the air, as if it wanted to jump back into Shelley's juicy mouth. She kept her distance, teasing him, merely tickling the top of the circumcised dome with the very tip of her tongue. Impatiently, he thrust his hips forward, pushing his cock closer to those ripe red lips. Shelley tantalised him for a few seconds more before finally relenting and taking the stretched-out weapon back in her mouth. Sliding her lips over its bulging head, she sucked at it like a fruit lollipop.

Miles felt his balls begin to quiver and twitch. The movement passed into the shaft of his cock, making it jump erratically. Feeling the pulsing between her sensitive lips, Shelley knew the time had come and plunged her head forward again, letting his beautiful cock slide into her mouth and throat. Miles began to shiver from head to toe as he looked down to see her ripe lips wrapped so tightly around the thick base of his cock and felt the swirling ministrations of her tongue upon its sides and tip. His knees buckled slightly as a wave of indescribably glorious sensation pulsed out from his sperm-filled balls and tore through his gut. He came then, with a yell of triumph, shaking his cock from side to side in Shelley's mouth as his come spurted out in a series of fast and violent pulses.

Shelley sat back on her haunches, grinning quite literally like a cat with the cream. She looked up at Miles with a devilish glint in her eyes, making a great show of rolling his sperm around in her mouth before finally swallowing it down in a single, greedy gulp.

She rose to her feet slowly. 'You can finish shaving now,' she said generously. 'And then I have something to tell you.' Leaving him to his ablutions, she sauntered back into the main room and perched herself on the bed.

Washed, finally shaved and clad in a white silk shirt with mustard-coloured St Rouchet slacks, Miles came in to join her, glancing nervously at his watch. A man who learned by his experiences, Miles wisely kept his distance. The previous night had taught him that Shelley was a predatory and dangerous animal – especially when on, or anywhere near, a bed.

'So, what did you want to tell me?' he enquired cautiously.

Shelley regarded him with a secretive smile on her face. 'Remember I told you about that friend of mine – the one who collects girlie films?'

Miles nodded. 'What about him?'

Shelley's smile became a triumphant beam. 'Well I phoned him early this morning – and guess what? He does a lot of business with this guy who distributes hot video films. You know, sex shops and back room, top-shelf stuff.'

It sounded interesting. Miles sucked at his cheeks thoughtfully. 'And?'

'This guy's looking for some new stuff, something really raunchy. He says there's some really big money in it.'

Money sounded even more interesting, Miles thought. He played it cool, sounding Shelley out. 'So what has all this got to do with me?' he asked warily.

Shelley shot him a scathing, almost pitying glance. 'I would have thought that was obvious. You shoot a film, making me the star, and I pass you onto my contacts. You get to make some big bucks, and I get to be in the movie business. Everybody's happy.' She fell silent for a while, gauging Miles' reaction. 'Well, what do you think?' she prodded him, at length.

Miles nodded thoughtfully. 'It sounds fair enough,' he admitted. 'But how raunchy does your friend's friend want his material, and how far are you prepared to go?'

Shelley nodded in the direction of the bathroom. 'I just showed you, didn't I?' she said, answering the second part of his question first. 'And as far as the film goes, any sort of bonking is OK as long as there's no suggestion of forced sex, child pornography or bestiality.'

Miles cast another anxious glance at his watch, feeling trapped by time. Shelley's proposition had him almost convinced, and he was sorely tempted to clinch some kind of an agreement there and then. But Amanda was waiting for him, and the Paradise documentary had to be his first priority. He decided that Shelley would wait. She seemed to have set her heart on appearing in a blue movie and probably wouldn't object too strongly to being pushed to the back of the queue.

'Alright, give me some time to think about it,' he said at last, hedging his bets. 'But right now I have to see Amanda and get her permission to film here.'

Shelley frowned, looking slightly peeved for a few moments. Quickly, however, her face cleared to give way to a slightly cunning smile. There was more than a hint of promise in her voice as she spoke. 'Maybe I could help to swing it for you,' she suggested. 'Amanda listens to me, and besides, she owes me a couple of favours.'

Miles raised one eyebrow fractionally. It was yet another snippet of potentially useful and interesting information, and thus worth thinking about. He studied the girl's face more intently, trying to read behind her eyes. Was she just bullshitting, he wondered, or did she really carry any weight with Amanda?

Shelley wasn't giving anything away, but she'd been doing a little bit of mood-reading too over the past few minutes, and it was pretty clear to her that she had Miles on the hook. The problem was, could she reel him in and land him? Perhaps it might help to make the bait just a little bit tastier, she decided.

'Just think about it, Miles – this could all come together very nicely,' she pointed out. 'With my help and my contacts, you could get to kill two birds with one stone. Use this place for both films and cut down on your location costs. Even better, you get to stay right here in the Paradise Club for a month or so – and I come with the room, if you want me.'

The implications were quite blatant and unashamed. It was also a pretty good offer, Miles thought, remembering the erotic thrill of Shelley's soft lips clamped around his cock and Sally and Freda's lascivious love-play. From a business point of view, it was even better. He had the location, a more than willing star, at least two co-performers and guaranteed sale and distribution for the finished product. All he had to do was to pull all the threads together.

He stepped over to the bed, kissing Shelley on the forehead and giving one of her beautiful tits a playful squeeze. There was a particularly determined sparkle in his eyes as he turned towards the door and headed off to keep his rendezvous with Amanda.

Chapter Nine

Amanda was not the sort of person to swallow any kind of bullshit, Miles had decided, being a fairly good judge of character. So he gave her the story more or less straight, although he played down the more obvious 'sexploitation' angle behind the intended series, projecting it more as a serious social documentary type of film.

Amanda listened attentively, and with interest. A couple of times, Miles thought he detected more than a passing spark of enthusiasm, and took it as a good omen. He finished his pitch on a high note, emphasising the positive aspects of wider publicity for the club.

'Well, what do you think?' he asked, after giving Amanda a few moments to digest it all.

Amanda looked genuinely sympathetic. 'I think it's a great idea,' she admitted. 'But unfortunately I can't give you the go-ahead. I signed an agreement yesterday with one of the tabloids, giving them exclusive rights to the Paradise story. One of the stipulations of the deal was that I don't allow any other branches of the media anywhere near the place.'

Up to that moment, Miles had been wearing a confident smile, sure that he had won Amanda over. Her refusal, even though she had it sound like a regretful one, hit him like a bombshell. His face fell.

Amanda immediately felt sorry for him. She racked her brains quickly, trying to find some way of cheering him up. 'Look, I'd like to try and make it up to you,' she said brightly, after a moment's thought. 'Tell you what – why don't you stay on here at the club for a few days, as my guest, with all the facilities thrown in? Then, if you like it, I'll give you a free life membership.'

It was a nice gesture – and an attractive offer, Miles realised – but it wasn't enough to make up for his disappointment. It was his turn to think quickly, going over all the angles. Amanda seemed quite genuine in her wish to compensate him. He couldn't help wondering exactly how conciliatory she was prepared to be.

It was Amanda herself who answered that question. 'Or if there's anything else I might be able to do for you,' she went on. 'Just let me know.'

One immediate thing sprang to mind, Miles reflected, covertly eyeing up Amanda's sensuous body – but he had bigger fish to fry. His earlier conversation with Shelley now sprang to the forefront of his thoughts. He had just lost the chance of a nice little earner, but there was still the possibility of salvaging the situation. He wasn't sure how Amanda would take to the idea, but now was definitely the best time to find out, while she was still in a conciliatory mood. Impulsively, Miles decided to go for broke.

'Actually, there was one other little project I had in mind,' he began. 'Your girl Shelley has already expressed a lot of enthusiasm and she thought you might be interested.'

Amanda was slightly on her guard, realising that she had put herself in a vulnerable position. 'Try me,' she muttered warily.

Miles paused to pull his thoughts into order, psyching himself up for another sales pitch. 'It seems to me that this entire place has a very special kind of magic,' he said eventually. 'A sort of atmosphere of fun, good times, lust for life.'

Amanda cut him short. 'Forget the life bit. Lust says it all,' she put in, with a grin on her face. 'Basically, what you're saying is that the Paradise Country Club positively reeks of sex.'

Miles felt strangely embarrassed. 'Well, yes,' he admitted sheepishly. 'Although I wasn't going to put it quite so bluntly.'

Amanda shrugged. 'Why not? Everybody else does,' she pointed out. 'I guess that's the attraction of the place. It *does* have a kind of magic – and it seems to affect everyone who stays here.' She paused for a while. 'So, what were you thinking of?'

It was time to grasp the bull by the horns. Miles summoned up inner reserves. 'I'd like to shoot another kind of film here. Not a documentary, a proper feature,' he said.

Amanda let out a small, silvery laugh. 'You mean a dirty movie. Why not just come straight out and say it? We're all grown-ups, you know.'

Miles managed a sheepish smile. 'We usually call them adult films,' he pointed. 'It's what you might call a trade euphemism.'

The fine distinction was lost on Amanda. 'So this is going to be our Shelley's crack at screen stardom, is it?' she asked.

Miles was caught a little off guard. 'She told you?'

Amanda nodded. 'She did mention something to that effect. Well, who could possibly stand in the way of a budding Linda Lovelace?'

Miles could hardly believe his ears. 'You mean you don't mind? You wouldn't object?'

Amanda laughed again. 'Why should I object? If you're going to make a sex film, what possible better place could there be to do it? But getting down to practicalities – exactly what's involved and how long would you need?'

Miles thought for a while. 'Well, I'd need a film crew of at least six on site,' he said after a while. 'Then there'd be up to eight other members of the cast and myself of course. As for time – say a week to set everything up and then another three to get it in the can. One month tops.'

Amanda frowned slightly. 'Doesn't seem long,' she pointed out.

Miles grinned. 'Hell, we're not talking about shooting a remake of Ben Hur. This is strictly low-budget stuff.'

Amanda was quietly fascinated. She had often wondered what was involved in film production, and now she had the chance to find out. 'What do you call low-budget?' she pressed.

Miles made a vague gesture with his shoulders. 'It depends, really. How desperate your actors and actresses are for work dictates how much you pay them. We don't usually bother much with standard Equity rates in this game. Then there's how much film you waste doing second takes, and the film crew's wages. I can usually bring in a forty-minute short for well under forty grand.'

Amanda thought about this for a while. 'But supposing

you weren't just thinking of a cheap short?' she asked. 'Say you wanted to make a full-length feature, something with a bit more class?'

Miles smiled rather wistfully at her. 'Ah, then we're talking about Happysville,' he muttered. 'Something I've always wanted to do – make a really classy sex film with a decent budget.'

'Then why not do it?' Amanda asked, simply.

There was a slightly dreamy look in Miles' eyes as he answered. 'If I could afford to finance it on my own, I would,' he said honestly. 'But I couldn't face that sort of an investment without a backer.'

Amanda was silent for a long time, thinking deeply. She'd been wondering what to do with the £25,000 the newspaper had paid for the Paradise story. The club itself was doing fine, and didn't need a cash injection. Rather than just blow the money away, Amanda had been thinking about some form of investment.

She faced Miles squarely, a businesslike look on her face. 'Just suppose I said that all your location costs are free,' she murmured quietly. 'I'll pick up the tab for all the food and accommodation for your cast and crew so that you'd all be right on site all the time. Wouldn't that help to cut out a lot of excess costs like travelling time and catering, and that sort of thing?'

Miles nodded. 'Yes, it would,' he admitted.

'And if I was willing to throw some extra money in? Say twenty-five thousand?'

The woman was serious, Miles realised suddenly. He faced her in a new light. 'Why would you want to do that?' he demanded bluntly.

Amanda shrugged. 'Let's just say that I wanted to diversify my business interests,' she suggested. 'I assume there's at least a reasonable chance of getting my money back – even making a modest profit?'

Miles nodded emphatically. 'Indeed, there's a very good chance,' he told her, in all honesty. 'The sort of film I'd be talking about sells pretty well on the home video market – and if they're good enough, there's the whole of Europe and the USA.'

It was exactly what Amanda had wanted to hear. She thought it all over for a few more moments, finally making up her mind.

'Alright – let's say we went ahead on that basis,' she said, still talking hypothetically. 'How does that look to you?'

Miles did a few quick figures in his head. They sounded good, he thought. Not what he would call a gigantic budget, but probably just about enough to shoot a reasonably good film if there were no major problems. He pursed his lips thoughtfully, turning his attention back to Amanda. 'I think we could probably do it,' he said.

Amanda smiled happily. 'Then let's do it,' she said impulsively. 'Let's make a porno in Paradise.'

Chapter Ten

The film crew straggled in over the next couple of days, creating an excited buzz throughout the club and quickly establishing their own particular little niche.

Andrew was particularly taken with Emily, the make-up and continuity girl. Although 'girl' was a business nomenclature, rather than an accurate biological description, Emily managed to effectively disguise her thirty-plus years with the tricks of her trade, achieving a direct-from-the-beauty-parlour look which belied her actual years. Short, plump and with breasts the size and shape of over-ripe watermelons, she reminded Andrew very much of a younger Sally, with much the same potential for sexual development.

For her part, Sally was immediately attracted to George, the chief cameraman. It was not so much his looks as his constant habit of clawing at the front of his corduroy trousers, transferring his prick from one side of his crotch to the other. To a woman who had studied such phenomena over the years, this indicated to Sally that the man's sexual equipment did not sit easily in his pants, suggesting healthy development rather than a poor choice of tailor.

Franklin, the set designer, was of no great interest to

anyone other than as a diverting side-show. Given to wearing blouson-type shirts in various shades of pink or yellow, he was so obviously queer as a tuppenny-clock that even Freda buttoned up her uniform whenever he was in the building. She had already set her sights on Charlie and Wayne, who handled lighting and sound respectively. A keen amateur electrician on top of her many other talents, Freda had already rewired the massage suite in preparation for the private *son et lumiere* show she was planning to hold at the first available opportunity.

Derek, the blond and impossibly good-looking second cameraman, was strongly fancied by everyone with the single exception of Andrew, who was secretly running a book on who was going to get his trousers off first. Currently, Amanda was running six-four favourite, although Franklin came a close second at even money. As Derek had yet to make a clear demonstration of his sexuality, Andrew thought he was on a pretty good bet to clean up.

No-one had seen much of Miles, who spent a lot of time locked in his room making alterations to the shooting script. This had been hastily commissioned from an elderly and semi-retired hack living in Bournemouth who was quite happy to churn out any sort of copy to order for the price of two bottles of Scotch a day. Well past serious bonking age himself, his highly raunchy material was largely made up from vague memories and unfulfilled sexual fantasies. However, Miles was now happy with the script and had finally come out of his seclusion to begin the job of casting.

The plot – not surprisingly concerning carnal activities in an unspecified English rural country club – required three male characters and an unlimited number of females. Miles had already retained the services of Sam and Melanie to back up his leading lady, and was hoping to include some footage of Freda and Sally to pad things out. It was the men who were causing the first serious headache – a little problem which he shared with Amanda over a lunchtime sherry.

'It's a bloody nuisance, really,' he moaned. 'I was planning to bring in Brett Robbins for the male lead, but the poor bugger's out of commission for a few weeks.'

'Good actor, is he?' Amanda enquired innocently.

Miles laughed, shaking his head. 'Brett couldn't act his way out of a paper bag,' he confided. 'But he's the best superstud in the business. Hung like a stallion, gets it up at a moment's notice and comes like the Trevi fountain.'

'So what's wrong with him?' Amanda wanted to know.

Miles shuddered slightly, pulling a face. 'Silly bastard caught the end of his prick in his zipper a couple of days ago. He's not going to be doing any close-ups until the scab heals over. I can't afford to wait, so I've had to get a few other guys to come down for auditions. They should be here later this afternoon.'

Amanda found herself wondering just what was involved in auditioning for a part in a porno movie, but decided not to ask. As it happened, she was soon going to find out anyway. Finishing her sherry, she made her excuses to Miles and left to socialise with the steady influx of other guests. News that the Paradise Club was to be the setting for a dirty movie had quickly got out on the grapevine and several regular members, including the formidable Bella, had checked in for an unspecified stay.

This unexpected bonus had not gone unnoticed by Andrew, who had got over his initially cool reaction and was warming quickly to the idea now that he could see the undoubted benefits for both business and pleasure. A virtually full club meant not only a boost in takings, but the opportunity for some good old-fashioned orgiastic activity. He was, in fact, laying the groundwork for such activity at that very moment, conducting Emily on a tour of the grounds and trying to size up her sexual potential.

'It's very good of you to take time off to show me round like this,' Emily gushed as they strolled past the tennis courts. 'I'm sure you're a very busy man, being a partner in a big place like this.'

Andrew was at his suave and charming best. He shrugged off her gratitude with a nonchalant wave of his hand. 'Only too happy to do it, dear lady,' he purred. 'Now, perhaps you'd like to see the outdoor swimming pool. We could even take a dip, if you like.'

Emily tried to look coy but didn't quite bring it off. 'But I haven't got a bathing suit,' she protested rather weakly.

Andrew managed to look both solicitous and gently mocking at the same time. 'Bathing suit?' he queried, as though it was some foreign term for which there was no direct translation. 'We never use those here. There's no shame in Paradise, you know.'

'Oh,' Emily said quietly. Her chubby face coloured slightly – although whether with embarrassment or the thrill of excitement, Andrew couldn't quite tell.

They had reached the poolside area. Andrew was pleased to notice that it was empty. Privacy was probably the single last thing he needed to break down any of Emily's remaining inhibitions.

'Well, how about it?' he asked, nodding towards the waters of the pool.

Emily looked tempted. 'It certainly does look inviting,' she conceded. 'And it is rather a hot day.'

It was time to put on a bit of pressure, Andrew thought. 'Well, I think I shall certainly take a quick dip,' he announced, stopping by one of the poolside tables and bending down to pull off his shoes and socks. He watched Emily's face out of the corner of his eye as he turned his attention to his shirt and pulled it off over his head.

He had got down to his underpants by the time she finally made up her mind. Andrew smiled inwardly as the woman's fingers strayed to the buttons of her blouse, toyed with them uncertainly for a few seconds and finally began unfastening them. Moments later, she had stepped out of a pair of blue cotton panties and was poised on the edge of the pool in all her naked glory.

Undressed, Emily was slightly plumper than Andrew had imagined. It was obvious that she chose her clothes well, going for a cut and style which had the maximum slimming effect. However, Andrew was not a great fan of lean and bony women anyway, so the general effect was still quite pleasing. Emily's arse was a trifle softer and wobblier than he preferred, but her large and pendulous breasts more than made up for this minor defect. She was definitely built for comfort rather than speed, Andrew thought.

'Well, here goes,' he said loudly, doing a passable running dive into the middle of the pool. Coming up and treading water, he looked up at Emily and grinned. 'Come on in – the water's lovely.'

Seeing Andrew happily splashing about made up Emily's

mind for her. Throwing caution to the wind, she stepped to the edge of the pool and jumped in to join him.

They both floated lazily for a while, their bodies not quite touching. Andrew wasn't quite sure what the next move was, let alone when to make it. He filled in time by admiring Emily's large, melon-like tits. With the buoyancy of the water holding them up and disguising their slight tendency to sag, they looked even more appealing. Soft, full and creamy, each swelling globe was tipped with a thick, fat nipple, surrounded by dark brown areolae the size of a two-penny piece. They were definitely tits which cried out to be fondled, Andrew thought, wishing that he was a bit more sure of his ground. There was absolutely no way of predicting how Emily might react if he made an open move. Until he had a more accurate idea of her sexual drive, he needed to proceed very cautiously indeed.

Andrew paddled in the water discreetly with his hands, moving his body tentatively towards hers. Kicking down beneath the surface, he stretched out one leg, probing with his toes until he made fleeting contact with her ankle. There was no obvious reaction. Andrew tried again, this time letting his foot brush against the back of the woman's calf for several seconds.

Emily had been waiting patiently for Andrew to show his hand. Not yet used to the ways of the Paradise, she had found him instantly attractive when they had first met, but not sure what his relationship with his wife actually was. She had accepted the offer of a tour round the grounds eagerly, certain that it would give her a chance to suss the man out more thoroughly.

Up to the point when they had both stripped off and

jumped into the pool, she still couldn't be totally sure that Andrew was making a pass at her or not. He was attentive and charming, certainly – but maybe that was just the way he was naturally with any woman. Not one to make the first move, Emily could only play the innocent and wait to see what happened.

The first touch of his foot might have been an accident, but the lingering stroke along the inside of her leg left no further room for doubt. Relieved that she did not have to play games any longer, she pushed herself through the water towards Andrew until their thighs touched.

There was nothing coy about her behaviour now. Emily fixed Andrew with a knowing, suggestive smile.

'I've never done it in a swimming pool before,' she informed him.

It was Andrew's turn to feign innocence – more out of surprise than anything else.

'What, swum?' he muttered, rather stupidly.

Emily giggled. 'Now we both know that we're not here to swim, don't we?' she said bluntly. 'But I think we'd be better off down in the shallow end.' With that she thrashed in the water, turning to face Andrew directly and pressing herself against him. With powerful strokes of her hands, she propelled him through the water until his feet made contact with the floor of the pool. Slightly taken aback by this sudden and unexpected turn of events, Andrew allowed himself to be pushed back until his buttocks were pressed against the side of the pool.

Emily stepped forward, her soft breasts mashing against his chest. Thigh to thigh, belly to belly, they both paused expectantly.

Andrew felt a delicious shiver of anticipation at the body contact. Through the cool of the pool water, the heat of Emily's flesh against his seemed particularly erotic. His cock began to throb gently. Reaching down, he retrieved it from where it dangled between Emily's legs and pushed it up between their bellies where it could stiffen more comfortably.

Emily was the sort of woman who liked a little romance with her sex. She thrust her face forward, lips pursed for a kiss. A gentleman as always, Andrew obliged.

It was not so much a kiss as a sudden explosion of passion. Emily's mouth clamped onto his, her soft lips sucking at his flesh. Her agile tongue snaked out and probed between his teeth, into his mouth and halfway down his throat.

It was as if the woman lived her entire waking life on the edge of complete abandon, primed for that first mouth contact as though it was a hair-trigger. Suddenly her entire body was a writhing, burning mass of flesh, pulsing with raw sexual energy. Her pelvis ground against his, her pelvic bone causing real physical pain as it hammered into his groin. Her huge breasts made wet smacking sounds against his chest as they rolled against him, alternately compressing then inflating again as she rocked her upper body from side to side.

Andrew was gasping for breath by the time Emily finally pulled her mouth away. Her eyes were glittering brightly, and her face was flushed and hot. Andrew could hardly believe the suddenness and sheer intensity of her arousal – particularly when all he had done was respond. He leaned back against the side of the pool apprehensively, waiting for the secondary assault.

It was not long in coming. Pausing only to get her breath back, Emily closed in for another kiss, her lips slavering over his mouth and nose in a warm froth of saliva.

Andrew's prick was fully stiff now, and Emily could feel its throbbing hardness against the soft flesh of her belly. With a little grunt, she pulled her hips back and reached down in the water to grab it in a firm grip. Pulling it out from his body at a forty-five degree angle, she climbed onto it, wrapping her chubby cunt lips around its bulging tip and impaling herself like a do-it-yourself kebab.

Totally bemused by the fury of the woman's passion, Andrew could only stand there as Emily quite literally swarmed over his cock, pushing her hot cunt down over its entire length. There was no slow build-up, no attempt to settle the stiff rod comfortably in her accommodating shaft. As soon as Andrew was safely inside her, Emily began to pump herself up and down his prick, fighting the buoyancy of the water by digging her sharp fingernails into the flesh of his buttocks to keep her in place. Dementedly, she rode him like a mechanical monkey on a stick which had gone out of control, grunting noisily with every stroke.

Andrew was amazed that a woman of Emily's build could explode into so much frenetic energy, and was forced to revise his earlier assumption that she would be the type for a slow, comfortable screw. What he was getting was a fast, furious fuck – and so far he had hardly moved a muscle himself.

All in all, he was feeling more or less superfluous to the entire proceedings. Emily's approach to sex was obviously completely impersonal – the man serving little other purpose than just being there. Andrew felt that he was no more than a masturbatory object, simply a stiff prick which the woman happened to be using to bring herself off. He felt vaguely angry, as if this were some kind of a slur on his manhood.

A cold rage built up inside him as Emily continued to pump herself up and down on his cock. Normally relaxed and laid-back in his attitude to sex, Andrew was now discovering a hidden sexual aggression in his psyche which he had never suspected existed before. He felt angry at this woman who was, to his mind, abusing his body. He needed desperately to fight back, perhaps not so much to exercise control as simply to let her know he was there.

His anger broke. Summoning his strength, Andrew pushed himself away from the side wall of the swimming pool, grasping Emily firmly by the hips and turning her round until he had reversed their positions. Savagely, he thrust her back into the very position where he had been, feeling her body jar as her soft rump slammed against the tiled side of the pool.

Teeth gritted, Andrew took over control, thrusting his pelvis forward and burying his stiff length in Emily's hot tunnel. Using the whole weight of his body against hers, he held her in place so that she was unable to move. Only when she had become completely still did he relax slightly, drawing back so that the tip of his cock was just lodged between her cunt lips, promising re-entry but denying it.

Emily seethed with frustration. Such was the frenzied nature of her love-making that she became completely and utterly swept up in it, so hell-bent on self-gratification that she had been almost oblivious to her partner. Now, having been abruptly stopped just when she was close to orgasm, it was like waking from a dream and being out of touch with reality.

She stared at Andrew's grim face blankly for a few seconds, not understanding what was happening. Then she became aware of his cock poised at the entrance to her aching cunt and her desperate hunger returned. Her pendulous bottom lip trembled as she regarded him through imploring eyes.

'Fuck me Andrew,' she whimpered pathetically. 'Give it to me.'

Andrew's anger had subsided now, to be replaced by a cold ruthlessness. He was back in control, a man again. And Emily wanted *him*, not just his disembodied cock.

He nodded faintly. 'Yes, I'll fuck you,' he told the woman. 'But I'll fuck you *my* way.'

Suiting his actions to his words, Andrew pushed forwards, sending his prick gliding smoothly up her sheath. He withdrew again slowly, treating himself to the pleasure of having his cock caressed and stroked by a thousand folds of slippery flesh.

Emily moaned, aching to thrust herself back on the welcome hardness of Andrew's prick, but afraid to do so. He had made it perfectly obvious that he wanted dominance, total control of the pace of their carnal union. Desperate for his cock to satisfy her, she dared not risk upsetting him again in case he abandoned her completely. Against all her natural impulses, she forced herself to remain completely submissive as Andrew jerked into her again, driving his rigid shaft home like a well-greased piston.

Again, he withdrew slowly and deliberately, increasing Emily's sense of frustration. She found herself wondering whether Andrew was choosing to tantalise her this way for his own pleasure or simply to teach her a lesson. Either way, it was having the strangest effect upon her mind and body. She could not remember ever feeling quite so hungry before, or having had the time to fully appreciate such an exquisite mingling of sensations. Each time Andrew plunged into her she was filled with tingling pleasure, only to suffer delicious pain as she lost him again.

Sensing the effect his technique was having on the woman, Andrew kept up his slow and lazy rhythm for several minutes, alternately sliding his prick the length of her juicy vulva and then pulling back to the point of near-withdrawal. Emily's whole body was a blubbery mass of twitching, nervous energy now as her lust built to a frenzy. Her huge breasts jiggled furiously on the surface of the pool, her hands and arms thrashed wildly in the water. A constant babble of strange, animal-like noises poured from her loose lips and sagging mouth – a mixture of grunts, sighs, gasps for breath and half-formed words. The sexually aggressive harridan was gone now, to be replaced by a desperate, hungry and totally helpless woman, who was completely at Andrew's mercy.

Knowing that she was tamed, that she needed him, Andrew finally relented. He slammed into her again, driving his prick deep into her cavernous, sucking hole. Bucking his hips, he rammed into her with short, driving strokes which made their bellies slap together wetly and churned the surface of the pool water into foam.

Emily jumped from her plateau of repressed lust into almost immediate release. Her guttural utterings changed to a low, continuous moan which began to rise in pitch until it was a single, unbroken scream.

Emily's body went limp, her legs buckling beneath her. For a moment, Andrew thought she would slip beneath the surface of the water. Not wanting to have a drowning woman on his hands, and close to his own orgasm, he propped her up by the simple expedient of grasping her large, soft tits and held her against the pool wall until he had finally pumped his full load into her cunt.

Afterwards, he towed her to the shallow end like a stricken whale and let her float in the water, her rounded arse bobbing gently up and down against the bottom of the pool. Pulling himself up onto the steps, he sat there patiently as Emily finally recovered herself enough to drag herself out of the water beside him. She was silent for several minutes, recovering her breath and composure. Finally, she turned to face him with a grateful look in her eyes.

'I'll tell you one thing,' she muttered breathlessly, 'your way's better.'

Chapter Eleven

Back in the club, the three hopeful male porno stars had arrived, and were awaiting their audition. Not quite sure what to do with them, Amanda had told them all to wait in the main bar while she went in search of Miles.

She finally tracked him down in the room she had allocated to Sam and Melanie. All three were sprawled out naked on the waterbed, and the wet, glistening condition of Miles' soft cock left little doubt as to what they had been doing.

'Rehearsals, or the modern-day version of the Hollywood casting couch?' Amanda enquired sarcastically.

Miles grinned sheepishly. 'Something like that.' He reached over the side of the bed for his pants and pulled them on. 'So, what's up?'

'Your trio of super-stud wannabes have arrived,' Amanda informed him. 'They're waiting in the bar.'

Miles finished dressing. 'Well, what do you think of 'em?' he asked, as he zipped up his slacks.

Amanda shrugged. 'Who knows? They could be ideal for a remake of a Marx Brothers movie for all I can tell.'

Miles grinned. He turned to Sam and Melanie. 'Well shake your arses, girls,' he urged them. 'It's audition time.'

He returned his attention to Amanda. 'I think it's only right you have a say in this as well. You are my principal backer, after all.'

Amanda looked dubious, not at all sure what was involved. Seeing the doubt on her face, Miles smiled reassuringly. 'Relax – I just want your opinion, that's all. Sam and Melanie here will put them through their paces if need be.'

Amanda glanced at the two girls, who seemed quite happy with this arrangement. It must be all part of the job, she assumed. She waited until the girls had dressed again and then followed Miles down to the bar.

The three auditionees jumped to their feet as Miles and his little entourage entered the room. They formed themselves into a neat line, displaying themselves like a row of carcasses in a butcher's shop window.

Miles treated them in much the same way. Not bothering to ask their names, he merely addressed Amanda, Sam and Melanie.

'Well, ladies – what do you think?' he demanded.

Melanie stepped forward, walking slowly along the line of men and eyeing them up closely. Finally, she turned back to Miles, wrinkling her nose in a faint gesture of disgust.

'Well none of them's Richard Gere, that's for sure,' she announced scathingly. 'Are you sure we can't afford to wait for Brett?'

Miles shook his head. 'Sorry, my darling,' he muttered regretfully. 'But until his dodgy dick heals up, Brett's out of the running.'

'Maybe we could cover the damage up with make-up,' Sam suggested hopefully.

Miles shot her a deprecating glance. 'Oh, great idea,' he

muttered sarcastically. 'I'm trying to shoot a blow-job in close-up, and my leading ladies have Leichner number seven dribbling down their chins. Besides, it would taste awful.' He turned his attention to Amanda. 'Come on, let's have a realistic assessment. Which of these three hunks would you like to see most in a dirty movie?'

Amanda allowed herself a wry smile. 'That really depends what they've got to offer, doesn't it?' she pointed out.

Miles nodded. 'Yes, well – that's the next part,' he told her. 'Just for the moment, I was merely thinking of immediate visual appeal.'

Amanda took another look, running a critical eye along the line. They were all passably good-looking, she had to admit – but none of them seemed to radiate any particular sex appeal. Finally, she looked at Miles again and shook her head hopelessly. 'I don't know, Miles,' she admitted.

Miles sucked at his teeth for a while, looking at Sam and Melanie in turn as though expecting some further input. Both girls were silent. Finally, with a deep sigh, Miles turned back to the men.

'OK, it's crunch time,' he announced. 'Get 'em off.'

The three guys obeyed meekly, all unhitching their trousers without a murmur and letting them drop to the floor. Like a well-choreographed chorus line, they pulled down their underpants in unison and exposed their limp dicks to public gaze.

Miles nudged Sam gently. 'Do you want to do the honours?' he asked.

The girl shrugged faintly. 'Yeah, sure,' she muttered, without any great enthusiasm. Walking across to the first guy in the line, she dropped to her knees on the floor in front of him. Cradling his soft cock in her hand, she pulled it towards her mouth and began licking it in a brisk, businesslike fashion.

The man's organ began to swell immediately. Sam gave it an experimental squeeze as it hardened into full erection, then shuffled along to the next in line and delivered the same treatment. Finally, when all three cocks were standing proudly to attention, she climbed to her feet again and withdrew to join Miles.

'Well, that's the best I can do,' she announced. 'And if you want a personal opinion, the guy in the middle comes up fastest and feels like he has a hard-on which is going to last. The first guy isn't too bad, but his cock's bent like a banana. The one on the end just hasn't got the meat. A five-incher at the most.'

Miles digested this assessment quietly for a few seconds, before stepping forward to examine the three erect pricks for himself. Completely ignoring the feelings of their hapless owners, he called over his shoulder to Sam.

'You're right about the one on the end,' he confirmed. 'Not enough to make your cheeks bulge – and our customers do like bulging cheeks.'

He tapped the owner of the five-inch prick on the shoulder. 'You can go,' he said cold-bloodedly. 'Sorry, but we can't use you.'

The man in question flushed red with embarrassment and stared abjectly down at his own feet. Looking totally dejected and miserable, he pulled up his pants and trousers and walked out of the bar without saying a word.

Miles called for Melanie to join him. 'Right, give me your opinion of these two,' he said.

The girl reached for each cock in turn, hefting it in the palm of her hand and squeezing it as though testing for ripeness. Unable to make up her mind, she stood between the two young men and took their cocks in both hands, sliding her fingers up and down each stiff shaft.

'Yeah, Sam's right,' she confirmed at length. She nodded at the man on her left. 'They're both about the same in length, but this one's got better shape. Personally, I'd like another couple of inches, but guess he'll do at a pinch.'

Miles gave the matter a few more moments of careful thought before coming to a decision. 'OK, you got the job,' he called to the girls' joint choice. 'What's your name, by the way?'

The young man beamed happily. 'George – George Plunkett,' he said eagerly.

Miles frowned and pulled a face. 'That won't look good on the credits,' he mused. He was silently thoughtful for a while, finally brightening. 'OK, from now on your name's Dirk Scabbard,' he announced. 'And if anyone asks, you were born in Amsterdam from a Swedish strip-tease dancer and a French merchant seaman. Got it?'

The newly-christened Dirk nodded enthusiastically. 'Got it, Mr Lansing. You won't be sorry – believe me.'

The owner of the banana-shaped prick spoke for the first time. 'What the fuck am I supposed to do?' he demanded petulantly. 'Don't I even get my rocks off as a consolation prize?'

Miles shrugged. 'That's down to the girls,' he told the man. He turned to Sam and Melanie. 'Well, do you fancy giving our new star and his friend a little test run?'

The two girls exchanged doubtful glances, making it patently obvious that they weren't exactly thrilled with the idea. Finally, Melanie aquiesced with a faint shrug of her shoulders. 'Well, I suppose there's no point in letting a stiff cock go to waste – even if it does look like something in a greengrocer's window.' Licking her red lips, perhaps in anticipation of banana-flavoured come, she began to advance upon the cock in question. Following Sam's earlier example, she wasted little time with formalities, sinking down on her haunches and bringing the stiff, curved tool up to her mouth.

The young man's sullen expression began to fade, as Melanie's soft lips closed over the swollen end of his prick. However, he was still just a trifle disgruntled. He looked down at the girl avidly gobbling at his tool with the faintest look of rebuke on his face. 'By the way, my name's Rupert, just in case anyone's the slightest bit interested,' he pointed out.

Melanie said nothing, it having been impressed on her since childhood that nice girls didn't talk with their mouths full. Besides, she had to concentrate upon the tricky problem of getting a curved cock to slide neatly into her throat.

It was time to make a discreet exit, Amanda thought. Rupert seemed to be getting his consolation prize and Sam would probably need a bit of privacy to put Dirk through his paces. Pausing only to mention to Sam that the two young men could use the facilities of the club for the rest of the day, she moved towards the door, with Miles close on her heels. Outside, in the corridor, they fell into step together, Miles treading with a heavy, world-weary step.

He seemed far from happy, Amanda thought. 'Problems?' she asked, in a friendly fashion.

Miles nodded morosely. 'It's our friend Dirk,' he muttered. 'He isn't really what I was looking for. He'll do for
long-shots, I suppose, but he hasn't got what it takes for
close-up stuff.'

Amanda was sympathetic. 'Can't you just get someone
else?' she asked.

Miles sighed. 'It looks like I'm going to have to – but
where? I can hardly put an advert in "Stage" magazine –
WANTED – white male with nine inch prick.'

Amanda was thoughtful for a while as a sudden idea
struck her. 'Is that really the sole requisite for a leading
man?' she asked finally. 'An oversized cock?'

Miles nodded. 'More or less. I mean, dammit – we're not
going to need the guy to play King Lear. But, like I said,
real superstuds aren't too common, even in this business.'

Amanda started to grin triumphantly, fishing in the
depths of her shoulder-bag. 'I think I might be able to help
you out there,' she announced, pulling out John's business
card and handing it to him.

Miles read the card dubiously. 'A bra salesman?' he
queried. 'Doesn't sound very promising to me.'

Amanda shrugged the objection aside with a knowing,
secretive grin. 'Don't worry about what he does for a living.
He's got everything you could possibly need, take my word
for it.'

Miles started to brighten up. 'Really well hung, huh?' he
asked, sounding interested.

Amanda nodded emphatically. 'Biggest I've ever seen,'
she assured him. 'From what you've told me about Big

Brett, John could make him look like a two-year-old gelding.'

Miles was beginning to look really enthusiastic now. Momentarily, however, his face clouded over again.

'Mind you, he can't be too expensive. We can't really afford to pay him much.'

Amanda laughed. 'Don't even worry about it. If he's running true to form, he'll probably want to pay us.'

Miles seemed happy at last. He threw his arm around Amanda's shoulder, hugging her. 'Miss Redfern – you're a real find,' he announced jubilantly.

It was their first real body contact. With a slight shiver of pleasure, Amanda decided that she liked it.

Chapter Twelve

It was not in Sally's nature to be jealous, but she had a very keen sense of fair play and respect for the rules of the game. And the game she had played with Andrew for the past twenty-odd years had been essentially the same, the rules infinitely flexible and yet totally rigid in one single respect. No involvement.

Now Sally had a sneaking suspicion that this cardinal rule might have been broken, and it made her feel extremely vulnerable.

There were several reasons for her suspicions, not the least of which involved Andrew's general behaviour ever since he had taken Emily for a guided tour earlier in the day. Not only was he walking round with a particularly smug and self-satisfied grin on his face, he had also taken to singing aloud to himself – something which he had never done before. On top of this, his repertoire seemed to consist of only one song, and Sally had lost count of the number of times she had caught her husband trilling the chorus of *I Did It My Way*.

This, added to the fact that Emily appeared to be following him around like a labrador puppy, formed the basis for Sally's fears. An intelligent woman, it had not escaped her notice that in physical appearance, Emily was very much a younger version of herself. Knowing Andrew's penchant for the plumper woman, and his particular weakness for large, swelling tits, Sally could not help seeing the woman as a threat. Although Andrew had actually been in a state of mid-life crisis since the age of twenty-seven, he was now fast approaching his fifty-fifth birthday, and at what people described as 'that dangerous age'.

The danger of course being that he could imagine himself getting into a serious relationship with the younger woman. And whilst Sally could hardly resent her husband enjoying a quick bonk after her little adventure with Miles, any suggestion of a full-blooded affair was a definite no-no.

The problem was, she thought, what was she going to do about it? Calling upon her considerable feminine wiles, Sally developed a rather cunning little plan, the nub of which involved getting all three of them together. Anxious to put it into effect as soon as possible, she went in search of Emily.

Andrew, of course, knew nothing about Sally's suspicions. Had he done so, he would have very quickly put paid to them. In fact, although his session with Emily had been a great boost of his male ego, and he found the knowledge that she was obviously smitten with him rather flattering, he had absolutely no intention of repeating the experience. On the contrary, he had been going out of his way to avoid the young woman – which accounted for the way in which she had been following him around, desperately trying to renew contact. So Sally had actually got hold of the completely wrong end of the stick, and the insidious little plan she was currently cooking up would inevitably backfire on her rather unexpectedly.

For her part, Emily was highly conscious of the fact that Andrew was a married man, but had no concept of the strange nature of his actual relationship with his wife. However, she had convinced herself that he was totally infatuated with her and was only waiting for another opportunity to get her alone. So she was treading an extremely cautious path, trying to corner Andrew but stay out of Sally's way at the same time.

It was a totally bizarre situation. Three people, each with completely wrong ideas about each other, buzzing around within the pressure-chamber atmosphere of the Paradise Club and each being stalked by the very person they were trying to avoid. Like Sulphur, Carbon and Potassium Nitrate, the three elements of gunpowder, they were safe only as long as they stayed well apart. If ever they came to mix together, there was almost certain to be one hell of an explosion!

Rupert wandered along the corridors of the club in the direction of the massage suite, still wondering if Melanie had been winding him up about Freda's extraordinary talent for straightening out bent cocks.

The girl certainly appeared to have been sincere, he thought – and her assurance that the Swedish masseuse could straighten out anything that was made of flesh or bone had given him new hope in life. Quite apart from preventing him enjoying the job satisfaction of a career in porno movies, the unfortunate curvature of his cock-shaft was a constant source of ridicule and shame. Not the least part of his discomfiture was a sense of guilt that it was all his own fault, having been a fervent and frequent wanker between the ages of eleven and seventeen. Too late, Rupert had realised that he should have changed hands from time to time, to prevent his maturing prick adjusting itself permanently to the grip of his right fist.

He eventually found the massage suite and hovered outside the door for a few moments, steeling himself for what was bound to be an extremely embarrassing encounter. Not being used to the ways of the Paradise Club, he knocked loudly on the door before entering.

It was a sound Freda had not heard in many a month. She glanced up in surprise. 'Come,' she called out, enjoying the chance to use one of her favourite words.

Rupert edged nervously into the room, not knowing quite what to expect. He was totally unprepared for the sight of a half-naked blonde Amazon who looked more like an over-developed Gladiator than a female masseuse.

Freda regarded him with benign interest. He was male, he was young, and he was passably good-looking. Three out of three wasn't bad, she told herself.

'Ja?' she enquired politely.

Rupert found himself tongue-tied suddenly. The little speech he had so carefully rehearsed refused to emerge. Finally, his words came out in a rushed, nervous babble.

'Melanie told me that you have a revolutionary massage technique for straightening out deformed joints and muscles and suchlike,' Rupert blurted out. 'So I was wondering if it would work on my prick.'

The complexities of the English language had never been one of Freda's strong points. At best, she perhaps understood one word in four, and then only when they were spoken slowly and with great emphasis. So Rupert's little speech might as well have been delivered in Serbo-Croat. There were, however, two familiar words which she had managed to pick out. They were 'massage' and 'prick'.

She fixed Rupert with a broad, beaming smile. 'You want I massage prick?' she asked, hardly believing her luck.

Not knowing how bad the Swedish girl's comprehension actually was, Rupert assumed that she had got the general idea. He nodded awkwardly. 'The thing is, you see – it's bent,' he went on to explain.

The smile disappeared from Freda's face. Along with most popular cuss-words and obscenities, several bits of English slang had also filtered their way into her limited vocabulary over the years. Among them was the word 'bent' – which memory told her had something to do with men who preferred sticking their pricks up other men's bums. Or, conversely, having pricks stuck up theirs.

She stared at Rupert in some confusion. 'You . . . bent . . . but want I massage prick?' she asked uncertainly.

Rupert nodded eagerly, feeling relieved that it was all going a lot easier than he had imagined. Had he been less euphoric, he might have taken warning from the black look which was stealing across Freda's face.

Glancing across the room, his eyes fell on the massage table. He skipped across to it, speaking to Freda over his shoulder. 'I expect you want me to get my clothes off and lie down here while you get things ready,' he said chattily, doing exactly that without waiting for an answer. Naked, he lay on his back waiting expectantly.

Freda fumed inwardly, both from a sense of disappointment and the indignities of her job. Not only had she been cheated out of a nice young cock to play with, she was now expected to prostitute her calling by administering treatment to a man who preferred his own sex. However, the terms of her employment at the Paradise Club called upon her to cater to a wide variety of tastes, and Freda was prepared to put up with quite a lot just for the occasional sexual perk which the job provided. Buckling down to it, she strode purposefully over to the wall cupboard and took out the supplies and equipment she figured she would need.

She walked back towards the supine Rupert holding a pot of massage cream, a small jar of petroleum jelly and a large, phallic-shaped device.

Rupert regarded this last object with fascination. A young man of surprisingly sheltered background, he had never actually seen a dildo before, let alone understand what they were used for. He could only assume that it was some kind of external splint which would be placed over his own organ to help the straightening process. Admiring the dildo's admirable stiff shape and impressive dimensions, Rupert felt quite excited at the prospect. If his own organ could be trained to even approximate it, he would be more than satisfied and his career in blue movies would be assured.

Freda stood over him, her face impassive. He smiled up at her. 'All ready to begin now, are we?' he asked.

Freda gave a curt nod. 'Ja. You are turning onto side, pliss.'

For some reason, Rupert had assumed that the treatment would be delivered while he was lying on his back. Nevertheless, he did as he was told, certain that the woman knew exactly what she was doing. So far, she seemed remarkably efficient, he thought.

'Relax, pliss,' Freda commanded. Rupert obeyed,

drawing in a long, deep breath then exhaling slowly and imagining any tension flowing out of his body as he did so.

Freda moved into position at his back. Then, pausing only to slap a large dollop of petroleum jelly between the cheeks of his arse, she flexed her powerful wrist and eased the dildo deeply into his anus.

Completely unprepared for this sudden penetration of his virgin arsehole, Rupert's entire body jerked into rigid, frozen tension. There was a momentary silence before his scream of surprise broke, filling the massage room as though all the demons of hell had suddenly broke loose.

Freda ignored the outburst. She was, after all, fairly used to screams in her profession. Anxious to get the unpleasant job over as quickly as possible, she merely switched on the dildo's internal vibrator and skirted round the massage table to Rupert's front side. Rubbing a thin film of massage cream into her hands, she reached for the young man's limp cock.

Rupert's rigid body relaxed slightly as the initial outrage subsided. Not quite sure what was going on, but still trusting the Swedish girl to know what she was doing, he lay there passively as the vibrating dildo buzzed away happily inside his rectal passage. Freda's warm, slippery hands caressing his prick were a consolation, and he soon felt himself responding to her touch. His dick swelled into hardness, and was soon throbbing stiffly between her agile fingers.

It was at this moment that Sally chose to burst, unannounced, into the massage room. She stared at the recumbent Rupert, who apparently had a stiff prick protruding from both sides of his groin, then cast a querulous glance at Freda.

The Swedish girl hastened to explain. 'Him bent,' she muttered, nodding down at the young man on the table. 'But like prick massage.'

For the first time, Rupert felt a sneaking suspicion that all was not quite as it should be. It certainly seemed as if Freda suffered from certain limitations of language, and there had to be a reason for the look of contempt which had crossed Sally's face at the last announcement. Slowly, he began to understand. He looked up at Sally appealingly, hoping that she would be some use as a translator.

'For Christ's sake,' he blurted out. 'Tell her it's not *me* that's bent – just my prick.'

Checking this statement out, Sally studied the stiff cock which Freda was masturbating briskly. There was no doubt about it, the engorged organ definitely had a slight curvature which gave it a banana-like appearance. She looked Rupert in the eye, sympathetically.

'Oh dear,' she murmured quietly. 'It does look as though Freda has got hold of the wrong end of the stick. Or in this case, the prick,' she added, unable to resist the joke.

It was not appreciated by Rupert, who glowered up at her. 'Why weren't you here five minutes ago?' he demanded petulantly.

Sally switched on her look of sympathy again. She jabbed her thumb towards the dildo, which was still throbbing away in Rupert's arsehole. 'Would you like me to pull that out?' she enquired solicitously.

Rupert thought about it. The sensation wasn't entirely unpleasant. In fact, it seemed to lend a mild erotic thrill to the feeling of Freda's hand gliding up and down his cock.

'No, you might as well leave it there,' he muttered finally. 'I've sort of got used to it now.'

Sally shrugged, 'Please yourself.' She returned her attention to the young man's prick, studying it in greater detail. It really wasn't all *that* bent, she thought. Certainly not enough to detract from its overall length and general appeal. Indeed, it might make a pleasant change to wank a cock which seemed designed to wrap itself over one's fingers. She glanced up at Freda, who continued to rub the stiff shaft up and down with detached professionalism. Having missed most of the conversation between Sally and her client, she was still under the impression that she was wasting her time on him.

'Would you like me to take over?' Sally asked her tentatively, trying not to appear too keen.

The big Swedish girl shrugged her broad shoulders. 'Ja – is OK,' she muttered, letting go of Rupert's prick and letting it slap back onto his belly. She stepped back, making room for Sally to move in.

Sally wrapped her fingers around the thick stalk, sliding the outer skin up and down a couple of times experimentally. Slick and shiny from the application of massage cream, Rupert's cock moved like oiled silk. Warm to the touch, it felt rather nice.

'Slow or fast?' she asked Rupert politely. 'Which would you prefer?'

The young man was having a little difficulty coming to terms with the rapid passage of unusual events. It had finally dawned upon him that he was not going to get his prick straightened after all – although he did, apparently, now have the choice of masturbatory technique.

'Slow,' he said firmly. Having got accustomed to the dildo pulsing away in his arse, he was now beginning to quite enjoy the tingling sensation of pleasure its vibrations were sending into his groin. He might as well make the experience last as long as possible, he thought.

He relaxed as Sally followed his instructions to the letter and began treating his cock to a series of slow, gentle strokes. Almost immediately, Rupert realised that Sally's manual ministrations were completely different to those of the Swedish bombshell. Although the precise and expert touch of Freda's fingers reflected her professional expertise and training, they lacked the loving care which Sally was now lavishing upon his stiff tool. Where Freda had merely been doing a job, Sally was wanking him for pleasure, and really putting her heart into it. Rupert sighed dreamily, feeling his prick twitch happily in response to Sally's devotions.

She carried on for several minutes, falling into a lazy, relaxed rhythm. The massage cream anointing Rupert's prick began to dry up, becoming sticky. With a slight sense of annoyance, Sally realised that she was going to need further lubrication. Without breaking her stroke, she glanced around for the pot of cream, but it was gone. Having lost interest, Freda had busied herself tidying up and putting things away, and had retired into one of the private cubicles to amuse herself with Dick Double-Up.

Forced to improvise, Sally did the best she could. Rolling saliva around in her mouth, she dribbled onto the head of Rupert's cock with uncanny precision. At once it became slick and pliable again, and she jacked his pulsing tool with relish, gradually speeding up the tempo as Rupert's body began to twitch upon the table.

He came with a convulsive shudder, gushing his lust over her agile fingers. At last Sally let go of his cock and reached for a small towel, wiping her hand clean. Tossing it into Rupert's lap, she moved away from the massage table and without a word, went off to find Freda and complete the business she had come for in the first place.

That was obviously that, Rupert thought, rubbing his wilting prick with the towel. He reached round to his behind and unplugged the vibrator from his arsehole, switching off the motor. There seemed little else to do except get dressed again and leave.

He swung his legs over the side of the table, feeling a dull aching sensation in his rectum as he did so. Jumping down onto his feet, he moved towards his clothes, surprised to find that he was hobbling slightly. Bending down to retrieve his pants and trousers produced a distinct twinge of pain, and he began to regret asking Sally to leave the dildo in place.

Finally dressed, his arse throbbing and with his prick just as bent as it had been when he came in, Rupert limped towards the exit. He found himself wondering if there might be a future for him in homosexual porn movies.

Chapter Thirteen

Sally's master plan was nearly complete, having persuaded Freda to turn over the massage suite and disappear out of sight for a couple of hours. The theatre was booked, the play chosen and the stage set. Now all she had to do was to assemble the players.

She was wearing one of her most coquettish smiles when she finally tracked down Andrew. Sidling up to him, she stroked her hand up and down the side of his thigh playfully.

Andrew raised his eyebrows slightly, recognising the old come-on when he saw it. 'Feeling a bit frisky are we, old girl?' he asked, with a smirk on his face.

Sally nuzzled against him with the sensuous grace of a cat. 'Frisky is a bit of an understatement,' she purred. 'To tell you the honest truth, I'm feeling as horny as hell. I think I'm long overdue for one of our little games.'

Andrew's smirk became a broad grin. 'Well I'll go along with that, anytime,' he said enthusiastically. 'So what's it to be? A bit of bonking on the billiard table, or perhaps playing gee-gees in the gymnasium?'

Sally smiled mischieviously. 'Actually, I was thinking of a hot little session in the massage suite,' she announced. 'I just happen to know that Freda is out of the way for a couple of hours, and we haven't given each other a good rub-down for ages.'

Andrew's eyes glittered, liking the sound of things more and more by the second. 'Perhaps we could do that little number where we oil our bodies all over and do it on a towel on the floor?' he suggested.

'Or I could stretch you out on the vibrating manipulation table and ride you jockey-style,' Sally put in, seeing how enthusiastic Andrew was becoming. His eyes were flashing like car hazard lights, and his face was tinged with a hot flush.

He licked his lips greedily. 'Well then, what are we waiting for?' he stammered out. 'We don't want Freda coming back and spoiling the fun.'

Sally said nothing, smiling inwardly, knowing that her husband was well and truly hooked. He would find out about the second part of her plan soon enough. She followed Andrew dutifully as he turned eagerly towards the massage suite.

He started stripping off his clothes almost as he walked through the door, tossing them into an untidy pile on the floor in his haste. It had been quite a few weeks since Sally had been really horny, and he knew from past experience what delicious pleasures were likely to be in store for him. Naked, he hopped about on the floor like a cat on hot bricks, anxious for the fun to begin.

'Come on then, old girl – get 'em off,' he urged her impatiently, as Sally made no immediate move to undress.

Sally cast a covert look at her watch, noting that she needed to play for time for at least another couple of minutes. She flashed a lascivious smile in Andrew's direction.

'I'll tell you what – I'll do a striptease for you,' she suggested. 'Help you get warmed up.'

Andrew felt like telling her in no uncertain terms that he didn't need warming up, but played along for her sake. Sally obviously wanted a big show, and preferred a slow build-up. He nodded his agreement and scurried over to the massage table, hopping up on it to get a better view of the performance.

Stepping out into the middle of the room, Sally did a couple of quick loosening up exercises and launched herself into a slow and sensuous bump and grind routine. Cradling her plump tits in her hands, she rolled them around like huge mounds of play-dough beneath her blouse, pushing them forward so that her prominent nipples traced intricate patterns through the thin material.

She ran her hands down over her stomach and the fronts of her thighs, swaying her pelvis backwards and forwards suggestively as she did so. She pressed her skirt into her crotch, stretching the material apart with her fingers until her pubic mound was clearly defined. Then, stroking her hands back up her body, she began to pick at the buttons of her blouse, continuing to sway her body in a provocative fashion.

It wasn't exactly Gypsy Rose Lee, but Andrew found it exciting enough. His prick swelled into hardness as Sally exposed first one, and then both of her magnificent tits for his approval. She toyed with her prominent nipples, teasing them into erection.

There was a timid knock on the door. Sally hastily abandoned her routine and threw off the remainder of her clothing. She looked over towards Andrew with a deceptively innocent smile on her face.

'Oh, by the way – I invited Emily to join us,' she announced sweetly. 'It's fairly obvious you two are quite taken with each other, so I thought you'd enjoy the chance to play a threesome.'

Having delivered her little bombshell, Sally moved away to answer the door.

If Andrew was surprised, then Emily was absolutely dumbstruck. The message that she had received – through Shelley – was that Andrew wanted to meet her in the massage room. Eagerly expecting a quiet tryst with the man of her dreams, the very last thing she had expected was for the door to be opened by his naked wife. Caught completely on the hop, she could only gape open-mouthed at Sally like a hooked fish.

Sally beamed at her. 'Ah, Emily – do come in,' she gushed. 'I'm so glad you could join us. Andrew is going to think up a very special party game that we can all play together.'

Sensing that the woman might be about to turn and make a hasty getaway, Sally seized her by one chubby arm and hauled her bodily into the room, closing the door firmly behind her. Emily looked awkward and nervous, staring at Andrew with a pleading look in her eyes, almost begging him to extricate her from the embarrassing situation. Wide-eyed and open-mouthed, she reminded Sally strongly of a helpless heroine in an old black and white silent movie.

More for his own sake than from a sense of chivalry, Andrew hastened to the rescue. Having set his heart on an intimate and torrid session with his wife, he had a vested interest in getting rid of her.

'Look, maybe Emily doesn't really want to play threesome games,' he suggested. 'It might not be her scene.'

Sally swept the objection aside. 'Nonsense,' she said firmly. 'If Emily wants to be one of your regular little playmates, then she has to understand the rules of the game.'

She turned back to the nervous woman. 'Come along then, Emily,' she chided. 'The sooner you get your clothes off, the sooner we can all get started.'

Sally watched the young woman's obvious discomfort with satisfaction, feeling increasingly confident that her little scheme was working out more or less as she had intended. By throwing Emily in at the deep end, exposing her to an impromptu and totally unexpected sexual three-some, Sally planned to achieve two objectives. Firstly, by making the freewheeling yet oddly binding nature of her marriage to Andrew obvious, she hoped to convince the young woman there was no place for her in his life as a solo performer. The second part of the plan was flexible, depending how Emily reacted – but should work equally well either way. If the idea of group sex scared Emily off immediately, then all well and good. If, however, she played along and enjoyed the experience, then it bound her into a mutual conspiracy, effectively neutralising her as a threat.

At the moment, it was looking very much as though the first scenario was most likely. Emily was clearly embarrassed and unsure of herself, looking as though she wished the earth could swallow her up at that very moment.

It was time to put on a little more pressure, Sally thought. She smiled warmly at the nervous young woman, affecting an air of friendly concern.

'Perhaps you'd like Andrew and I to help you get undressed,' she suggested. She glanced towards her husband, who was still sitting on the massage table and trying to remain detached. 'Come on then, Andrew. Let's get Emily ready to play.'

Andrew's eyes narrowed. There was something in Sally's tone which rang faint warning bells inside his head. Knowing her as intimately as he did, he was finely attuned to his wife's moods and patterns of thought – and there was definitely some little undercurrent to the present situation which he did not recognise. However, Sally's clear instruction had been a command rather than a request, and something told him it would not be wise to ignore it. With a sense of resignation, he climbed down from the table and hurried over to do her bidding.

Up until that precise second, Emily had felt a sense of unreality, as though the bizarre situation could not possibly be happening. Was she asleep and in the throes of some strange erotic dream, she wondered. Or was she awake and the victim of an elaborate practical joke? The possibility that Sally might be deliberately tormenting her had also occurred. Perhaps the woman had found out about her illicit session in the swimming pool with her husband and this was her way of exacting punishment.

Now, however, she saw Andrew advancing upon her in response to his wife's bidding and realised that none of these things were true. The situation was exactly as it appeared to be – Sally and Andrew really did want to draw her into a sexual threesome, and she had a decision to make.

Sally stood at her side, and Emily could feel the heat of the woman's naked flesh through her clothing. Andrew was almost upon her, his hands already coming up to the level of her breasts, as though poised to tear her blouse from her body. At any second, the freedom to make that decision would be taken from her. Andrew and Sally would undress her forcibly and she would no longer have a choice. A feeling akin to panic swept through her, and she took a hasty step backwards, her eyes darting nervously from Andrew to Sally then back again.

Sally grinned with triumph. The woman was about to crack, she told herself. Any second now she would scream, turn away and run from the room. The game would be won.

But her self-congratulation was premature. Emily did not turn and run. Instead, her fingers rose to the top of her blouse, and her mouth opened not to scream, but to speak.

'Alright – I'll undress myself,' Emily blurted out, picking feverishly at the buttons. In seconds the blouse was undone and discarded, and Emily's hands were behind her back, unhooking the clasp of her bra and allowing her great melon-like breasts to swing free. Kicking off her shoes, she dropped her skirt and peeled off her panty-hose and knickers.

Sally's momentary disappointment passed as the younger woman's voluptuous figure was exposed in front of her eyes. It was a soft, pleasing body, which offered all sorts of delightful possibilities. Sally adjusted her mental attitude to make the most of the changed situation. The game had not been lost, merely subjected to new rules, and she might as well enjoy the playing of it.

Stepping forward, she seized the naked Emily by the hand and pulled her over to the massage table. Jumping up to sit on it with her legs dangling over the side, Sally urged the woman to join her then snuggled up close so that they were pressed shoulder to shoulder, thigh to thigh.

She called out to Andrew. 'Feast your eyes on all this delicious flesh, my love.'

Andrew was also adjusting himself to the game and becoming increasingly enthusiastic, now that Emily had shown herself willing. He looked over at the two women, admitting that his wife did have a good point. Pressed together, she and Emily made an appealing picture. Four huge, soft breasts to be admired and fondled, two sets of smooth, fleshy, creamy thighs, each broken only by a furry triangle of pubic hair.

He did exactly as Sally had suggested, feasting his eyes until looking was no longer enough. Striding over, he placed one hand on Emily's left tit and one on Sally's right, exploring their plump smoothness with his fingers and palms. He ran his hands together and back again, his thumbs flicking over two sets of firm nipples. Squashing all four breasts together into a warm and fleshy mass, he rolled them against each other, admiring the way that they wobbled and quivered at his touch.

His mouth felt dry. Andrew sucked up saliva from the back of his throat, moistening his palate and then running his damp tongue over his lips. He moved his head forward and licked slowly and luxuriantly along the row of four nipples, savouring the salty but distinctive taste of each woman's flesh.

It was an extremely pleasant sensation, and one worth repeating several times. Andrew rocked his head from side to side, running his lips and tongue to and fro along the line of nipples like a man trying to play an oversized harmonica. No sound emerged, but it was sweet music anyway.

Warming to his fun, Andrew realised that there was more to be enjoyed. Not just four soft tits, but two juicy cunts as well. He slipped his hands between Sally and Emily's thighs, rubbing his fingers down through the springy hair of their respective fannies. Probing in the clefts of the twin set of labial lips, he slid two fingers into each moist orifice.

Frigging both women gently with his fingers, Andrew returned his attention to their tits, perhaps his single greatest pleasure in life. He buried his face in warm flesh, licking and sucking and slavering from side to side like a dog with a choice of bones.

Much as she appreciated the feel of Andrew toying inside her steamy slit, Sally was hotting up for a bit more direct action. She eased herself to the very edge of the massage table and slid down over the side, causing Andrew's fingers to pop out of her cunt and trace a slippery trail of juice up her belly. She turned to Emily, pulling the woman forward so that she was poised on the very edge of the table and prising her thighs apart. Lowering herself to the floor, Sally sat upright between Emily's dangling legs, the top of her head more or less on a level with the table. She looked up at her husband with a lascivious leer on her face, framing her soft full lips into a sexy pout.

It didn't take Andrew long to get the idea. Grinning widely, he withdrew his fingers from Emily's cunt and reached for his prick, which was now stiff and throbbing. Holding the shaft firmly in his hand, he straddled his wife's head and guided the tip of his cock to Emily's gaping fanny.

She gave a little gasp of pleasure as Andrew slid the first

couple of inches of his stiff rod inside her. With a little push, Andrew gave her his whole length, burying his cock up to his balls. These being all there were left to play with, Sally took what was on offer. Tilting her head up, she stuck out her tongue and began to lap at the wrinkled underside of his scrotal sac.

His earlier session with Emily had taught Andrew that it drove her wild to be teased, and he used that knowledge to the full now. Pulling back his deeply embedded cock until the domed head rested against her quivering clitoris, he held it there for several seconds before withdrawing completely and offering it instead to Sally's greedy tongue.

Sally responded eagerly, sliding the blade of her tongue along the pulsing underside of her husband's prick-shaft, still glistening wetly with Emily's internal juices. With a little grunt of pleasure, Andrew returned to Emily, sliding his cock back into her welcoming sheath and making her whimper with delight.

He fell into a slow but regular rhythm, alternately transferring his prick from Emily's cunt to Sally's mouth. She had pulled her tongue back now, and presented her slightly parted lips instead as a welcoming receptacle for his juicy offering. This delicious fuck-and-suck routine went on for nearly ten minutes, with Andrew carefully pacing himself to stay at a peak of pleasure without becoming too excited. The two women, however, were primed to bursting point, each in their own chosen fashion aching to receive the benison of Andrew's creamy discharge.

With the constant transfer of Emily's slippery love-juice to Sally's lips, and her saliva back to the younger girl's fanny, mouth and cunt were almost indistinguishable now.

Just two sucking, ravenous holes each slurping wetly as Andrew plunged his cock back into their depths.

Unable to contain himself any longer, Andrew felt a churning sensation deep in the pit of his belly which announced his imminent orgasm. Unsure of which woman to give his sauce, he chose to let it happen randomly, quickening his pace and stabbing both cunt and mouth several times each second.

He came in Sally's mouth, giving her a brief moment to suck out the last of his tangy emission before stuffing his cock back into Emily's creamy love-tunnel before it wilted. Jabbing furiously, he held a semi-hard-on for just long enough to bring the woman to the point of climax – which she achieved noisily and with a frantic kicking of her legs.

He stepped back, his rapidly softening cock now dangling between his legs. Sally regarded it with a wry smile on her face.

'Well, it looks as though us girls are going to have to look somewhere else for action for a while,' she observed aloud, for Emily's benefit. Clambering to her feet, she jumped back up onto the massage table and slipped one chubby arm around Emily's shoulders.

She was quite unprepared for the woman's response. It was Emily's first experience of anything outside one-to-one, basic male-to-female sex, and it had blown her mind. Up to that point, sex had always been a purely physical thing, and her needs were so strong and so demanding that they left little room for anything else. In short, Emily had always fucked with her body, never her mind. Physically, she gave her all in the frantic pursuit of pleasure and release, but mentally she had remained almost detached from the sexual act itself. This experience was different. The mere fact that she had taken part in group sex for the first time was enough in itself to impress itself into her consciousness. That she had enjoyed it so much was another factor which could not fail to register. And, finally, there was the erotic thrill which accompanied the realisation that she had dabbled in the forbidden – and enjoyed it. All in all, Emily felt sexually stimulated in a way that she had never even suspected possible before, and it had opened the floodgates of a lifetime of repressed desires.

She had felt a faint sense of pleasure when Sally had first sat close to her, their warm flesh touching. That feeling had risen to a mild erotic thrill when Andrew had squeezed their breasts together, and become a wave of passion when they had shared his cock. Now, as Sally sat cuddling her, Emily felt a stab of sympathy towards the woman which went far beyond a sense of sisterly kinship. Sally's arm around her shoulder became the caressing touch of a lover, the gesture itself a mere prelude to an explosion of carnal passion.

The floodgates burst. With a passionate sob, Emily threw herself into Sally's arms, her lips and tongue seeking the older woman's soft mouth. Unprepared for the assault, Sally fell sideways on the massage table as Emily flowed over her like a tidal wave of flesh, her soft round body quivering with lust.

Emily's hot mouth closed over Sally's, her tongue snaking between her lips. The sudden weight of Emily's body had knocked the breath from Sally's lungs. Now, with the woman's mouth sealing hers and a thrashing tongue stuck halfway down her throat, she was desperate for air. Making strangled choking noises in her throat, Sally writhed beneath Emily's heavy body, trying to free herself. She kicked her legs frantically, her feet drumming on the surface of the table.

Mistaking all this for a display of unbridled passion, Emily redoubled her efforts. Manoeuvring herself between Sally's thrashing legs, she slid up the helpless woman's belly until their two pairs of tits were mashed together, and their two cunts fused together.

The massage table, sturdy as it was, had never been designed to cope with the frantic sexual strugglings of two plump women. It sagged suddenly at one end, then tilted over sideways to an angle of about sixty degrees. The two women rolled off and fell heavily to the floor, only Sally's well-rounded and padded rump saving her from injury.

The fall knocked the last ounce of fight out of Sally's body. Stunned, she could only lie helplessly spread-eagled on the floor as Emily swarmed over her, covering her face with passionate kisses.

'I love you,' Emily was muttering rapturously between kisses and gasps for breath. 'I've always loved you, but I never realised it before.'

Detached from it all, Andrew watched the scene unfold with growing fascination, realising that something was different but not quite able to identify what it was. He had seen his wife take part in pseudo-lesbian couplings many times before – but they had been essentially sexless, merely using another body which just happened to be female for physical pleasure. Sally making love with a woman was invariably much the same as making it with a man. The actual sex of the body was unimportant – the body itself just a living masturbatory object.

Emily, of course, lacked the experience or the sexual sophistication to understand such fine distinctions. As far as she was concerned, Andrew and Sally had offered her an introduction into a world of total sexuality in which all things were possible, and all things acceptable. She had dabbled in group sex and quite enjoyed it. Now she was exploring lesbianism, and finding that she enjoyed it even more. True to her nature, she could only throw herself into it wholeheartedly. The fact that Sally did not seem to be responding with the same fervour did not strike her as odd because she had no terms of reference. Perhaps that was what lesbians did, she told herself – one played the passive role and one made all the action.

Her part seemed to have been pre-determined for her – and she was more than happy to play it to the hilt. Her hands flew over Sally's soft and pleasing body, fondling her wonderful tits, stroking the rounded smoothness of her belly and thighs.

Sally was slowly returning to reality now, and becoming more conscious of what was happening. Emily's loving attention to her body was a sensual pleasure, nothing else. But, just like Andrew, she could not fail to be conscious of the fact that something new and different was in play here.

The game appeared to be the same, the moves identical. Sally had played it before with Freda, with several of Andrew's lady friends, and with many of the strangers who had flitted in and out of the peculiar sexual lifestyle they had shared over the years. Flesh was flesh, the feel of its vibrant heat a source of simple tactile pleasure. A body pressed against hers was just a body, be it hard and masculine or soft and female. When orgasm was the simple and single-minded goal, it hardly mattered whether it was brought about by dick or dildo. Only the feel of something stiff inside her cunt achieved the desired effect – and the result was equally satisfying. A large female nipple or a small male one were equally attractive to suck. Both felt warm and alive between the lips, both tasted of salty, living flesh, and both conjured up soothing recollections of the warmth and comfort of a breast-fed childhood.

Sally felt as though she ought to respond as Emily moved her body downwards, sliding her hot, wet tongue through the deep valley between her breasts. Fully conscious now, Sally felt the warm glow of bodily satisfaction as the young woman kissed her tits, flicked her tongue over her taut nipples and then sucked them like ripe fruits. Moaning softly, Emily moved again, her drooling mouth tracing a wet path down Sally's stomach, her tongue lingering briefly in the pit of her belly-button before gliding ever-downward, over the bulging mound of her *mons veneris*.

Yet something kept her responses in check, told her that there was a new and powerful dimension to what was happening to her. With a sense of apprehension, even fear, Sally suddenly realised what it was.

This was not, after all, the normal game. In fact, it wasn't even a game at all. Emily was not playing at being a lesbian in the same way that Freda and the others played. For her, at least, this was the real thing. She was making love to Sally with her body, her mind, and all her emotions.

Sally shivered as Emily's stiff little tongue teased her clitoris, probed between her moist cunt lips. The warm tingling of sensual pleasure which it sent through her loins was counterbalanced by a feeling of icy coldness in the pit of her belly. Struggling to make sense of it all, Sally suddenly realised that she was scared.

She glanced imploringly over at Andrew, but he was looking blank and confused. Emily's tongue burrowed deeper into her slit, triggering off a whole new wave of strange and conflicting emotions. She was alone and isolated, Sally realised – perhaps for the first time in her life. That isolation let in doubt and a sense of insecurity, and she knew that she couldn't cope with it.

Emily was sucking at her cunt like a ripe peach, burying her nose and mouth in the source of the sweet juice. Even her own glands were betraying her, Sally thought crazily, producing a response where there should be none. With another shudder, Sally realised that her little scheme had backfired horribly upon her, changing her from plotter to victim.

Something snapped inside Sally's head. Suddenly, she needed to run away from the fear, the unknown beast which was confronting her. Scrabbling against the floor with her hands like an animal caught in a trap, she managed to pull herself up into a sitting position. She lifted her buttocks, pulling her cunt away from Emily's sucking mouth and scrambled to her feet. Stooping down quickly to gather up her clothes into an untidy bundle, she turned and made a run for the door, pulled it open and ran, naked and sobbing away down the corridor.

Emily stared hopelessly after her, incomprehension and the pain of rejection showing clearly on her face. She climbed to her knees, trotting over to the open door with the forlorn air of a faithful puppy which has just been whipped for crapping on the hall carpet.

'But I love you,' she wailed pitifully after the fleeing Sally. 'I love you.'

Andrew still didn't fully understand what he had just witnessed, but realised enough to know that he, too, needed to get away from this place as quickly as possible. There was nothing he could possibly say to Emily, who had now crawled back into the room and was lying on the floor weeping quietly.

Following his wife's lead, he hastily gathered up his clothes and made a discreet exit.

Chapter Fourteen

John arrived two days later, in response to Amanda's intriguing telephone call. He could hardly resist, after being promised three weeks of free luxury accommodation in an exclusive country club, all the sex he could handle and the personal attentions of at least two beautiful and sexy young film actresses. It was, as they say, an offer he couldn't refuse, and well worth taking his annual leave for. The planned fortnight in Benidorm seemed a pale substitute in comparison, and Amanda had assured him that she would personally refund his deposit.

Having checked him in and given him time to shower and change, Amanda escorted him proudly into the gymnasium, which had already been set up as the main interior studio. She introduced him to Miles and the film crew with the air of a Hollywood mogul parading her latest star discovery.

Miles was not immediately impressed. He pulled Amanda to one side, a slightly worried frown on his face. 'You neglected to mention he was quite so *ordinary* looking,' he complained.

Amanda smiled confidently, refusing to let her enthusiasm be dampened. 'Trust me, Miles. A true prince in frog's costume. A human version of the Indian Rope Trick, take my word for it,' she assured him.

Miles was not convinced, but tried to see the bright side. 'Well, maybe Emily can do something with him,' he muttered hopefully. 'It's amazing what a little make-up can do.' He was thoughtful for a moment, finally addressing the assembled film crew in general. 'Where is Emily, by the way?' he demanded of them. 'Has anybody seen her lately?'

Derek, the second cameraman, raised one hand tentatively into the air. 'She seems to have spent the last couple of days in her room moping,' he volunteered. 'I think something must have upset her.'

Miles rolled his eyes expressively, managing to convey the trials and tribulations of every film-maker in the entire universe at having to deal with the delicate temperaments of casts and crews.

'Do you want me to see if I can persuade her to come out?' Derek asked.

Miles shook his head wearily. 'No, let's get on with the audition.' He faced John directly, nodding over to the centre of the gymnasium floor. 'Right, get over there and drop your pants,' he snapped, in his usual matter-of-fact business tone.

John's face registered a look of shocked horror. He glanced nervously around the room, taking in the assembled gathering. Besides the film crew and Sam and Melanie, just about every other female on the club premises had managed to worm their way onto the set. News of John's super-cock had travelled fast, and no-one wanted to miss the grand unveiling. Safely behind the two cameras, Freda, Shelley, Bella, Sally and half a dozen other horny women were lined up against the wall-bars like the front row of a Chipperfield's concert, a look of glazed expectancy in their eyes.

Even Franklin had turned up, although his presence was not strictly necessary just for an audition. Wearing a rather fetching little red bolero top and a pair of impossibly tight matador pants which showed off the contours of his arse to its best advantage, he ogled John hopefully.

Turning a bright shade of pink, John turned back to Miles imploringly.

'What, in front of all these people?' he croaked awkwardly.

Seeing his obvious embarrassment, Amanda attempted to go to his rescue. She clutched at Miles' arm. 'Believe me, Miles – an audition really isn't necessary,' she told him. 'I'll personally vouch for the quality of the goods if you like. There's no way you could possibly be disappointed.'

Miles might just have taken her word, but the conversation had been overheard by Melanie. Having heard rumours of a monster prick which could put even the famous Brett Robbins to shame, she jumped in quickly to save the day for herself and womankind.

'Come on, Miles – you know the rules,' she chided him. 'You made them, after all. Every hopeful has to go through a full and proper audition.'

The girl had a good point, Miles conceded. He could hardly make an exception to his own rules, just on Amanda's say-so. He glanced at her apologetically. 'Sorry, Amanda, but Melanie's right,' he murmured. 'That's the way we do things.'

Amanda conceded defeat without a fight. Secretly, she

couldn't wait to get another good look at John's mighty weapon herself. Besides, she thought, it would give her a chance to show everyone that she hadn't been bullshitting. It was her turn to convey apologies to John. She gave him a helpless little shrug. 'I'm afraid you'll have to do as Miles says,' she told him. 'But believe me, it'll be a lot better than you think.'

The man nodded morosely, realising that he didn't have much of a choice in the matter. Although Amanda hadn't gone into much detail about the reasons for his free trip, and he hadn't the faintest idea what was going on now, he tended to trust her. His earlier encounter with her had been extremely fruitful, and something told him that the promised three weeks of luxury living and free sex were somehow dependant on his flashing his prick for public gaze. Fighting to overcome his natural shyness, he moved into the centre of the gymnasium and started to peel off his trousers.

There was a sudden hush, broken only by the sounds of heavy, expectant breathing as John's trousers slid to the floor. Stepping out of them, he hooked his thumbs into the elasticated waist of his Y-fronts and pulled them down as far as his knees before letting them drop.

A minor buzz of protest rippled round the gymnasium as John's white shirt-front dropped down over his reputed treasure.

'Get that bloody shirt off,' Bella shouted out, speaking for every woman in the place. 'It's spoiling the view.'

Figuring that he had nothing more to lose at this late stage, John obeyed meekly, pulling his shirt over his head. Standing stiffly to attention, he paraded his wares to his expectant audience.

Amanda glanced up at Miles, noting the dubious look which crossed his face. 'Yes, I know it doesn't look like much in this state,' she hissed in his ear. 'But get one of the girls to get it up and you'll see what I mean.'

Miles shrugged, turning to Sam and Melanie. 'So? Which of you wants to do the business this time?'

Melanie grinned wickedly. 'If it's half the size we've been led to believe, perhaps both of us ought to have a go,' she suggested. Tugging Sam's arm, she led her out into the middle of the floor where they both stood regarding John's nether regions with a critical gaze.

Amanda whispered to Miles again, remembering her own experience and thinking she ought to pass on the relevant information. 'It does take a bit of work to get it up,' she confessed. 'I'm afraid that John isn't very good at producing hard-ons to order.'

Miles frowned again. Amanda's bra salesman was looking less and less like a budding porno star by the moment. Nevertheless, he was committed now, and it only seemed fair to give the man a chance. He called over to Sam and Melanie.

'OK girls – get your clothes off and give the guy a bit of a helping hand, will you?'

Realising that the two gorgeous girls were about to strip off right in front of him, John's embarrassed look was immediately replaced by a self-satisfied grin. His soft prick gave a perceptible twitch, which did not go unnoticed by the eagle-eyed Sam.

She turned her head towards Miles, her eyes sparkling. 'Hey, Miles – this guy's cock is alive after all. Maybe we're in luck.'

The two girls threw off their clothes in a brisk and businesslike fashion. Exchanging a quick glance and a wink, they silently agreed their strategy and went to work.

Hands on hips, they both stood directly in front of John and shook their upper torsos from side to side, making their full breasts swing and jiggle provocatively. John's delighted eyes followed the elliptical path of four coral-pink nipples until he felt dizzy. His grin became a smirk, his tool beginning to uncurl from its sausage-like shape.

Melanie and Sam ceased their sensual gyrations abruptly as John's cock began to swell into more generous proportions. The rate of growth was slow, but steady, and both girls could already see the remarkable potential. An excited little buzz ran through the ranks of the female spectators in the gymnasium, as the tube thickened. Hanging out from John's groin, and still swelling by the second, it bobbed gently up and down, pulsing with the flow of rising blood.

The dubious expression which had been on Miles' face was fading now, to be replaced by one of surprise. He turned to Amanda, sounding optimistic for the first time since she had introduced John.

'You know, I'm beginning to think we might really have something here,' he conceded.

Amanda's baby-blue eyes twinkled as she regarded him with a slightly mocking, yet triumphant smile. 'Oh ye of little faith,' she chided. 'I told you, didn't I? Now get the girls to really go to work and you'll see a minor miracle of nature.'

It seemed like good advice, which Miles responded to. He called out to Sam and Melanie.

'Time for a little hands-on experience, ladies. We seem to have a little way to go yet.'

The two girls exchanged another brief glance, concurring wholeheartedly with Miles' assessment. John's cock appeared to have come as far as it was going to with visual stimulation alone. Fat and meaty, there was still a pronounced droop in the base of its shaft, giving it the appearance of an under-inflated party balloon. And, as both girls well knew – the only thing to do with a soft balloon was to blow it up a bit more.

The two girls sank to their knees in unison, facing each other with John's cock between them. Shuffling closer, they both stuck out their tongues and began to lap at his dangling balls.

The effect was both immediate and electrifying. As though it had just received a blast from a powerful hydraulic pump, John's cock sprang into sudden and complete erection, jerking up to lie ramrod-straight against his belly. A gasp of admiration rippled round the gymnasium. Freda was moved enough to gabble something in her native language. Nobody understood the words, but the sheer awe in her tone made the meaning clear enough. Bella broke into a high-pitched, quavering moan, and would have dashed past the cameras there and then had she not been physically restrained by Shelley and Sally.

For her own part, Shelley was greatly tempted to assert her rights of seniority as the film's star, and demand an immediate take-over of Sam and Melanie's supporting roles. However, her desire for John's magnificent cock was tempered by an instinct for self-preservation. She still needed Miles on her side, and she wasn't sure if he had a jealous streak. Playing safe, she held back, consoling herself with the thought that she would get more than her fair share of the super-weapon once filming started in earnest.

Franklin merely turned slightly pale and shuddered exquisitely. Reflecting that you could have too much of a good thing, he turned towards the exit and minced away at high speed, clenching his sphincter muscles tightly.

Miles let out a little whoop of exultation and threw his arms around Amanda's neck, kissing her full on the mouth. 'Amanda my darling, you've come up double trumps,' he told her, before releasing her and turning excitedly to the two cameramen.

'Get those bloody cameras rolling,' he screamed. 'I want as much footage of this as I can get. Long shots, zoom-ins, close-ups and any other goddamned shots you can think of. Forget sound – we can dub in any grunts and slurps later if we have to.'

Having given his directions to the crew, Miles returned his attention to John and the two girls. 'The audition's over,' he bawled out. 'This is a full take, so go for it.'

Sam and Melanie were still a little overawed by the monster they had released, but they rallied to the call like the seasoned performers they were. Putting on their best camera faces – which consisted mainly of looking like two hungry, predatory felines – they set about giving all for the sake of their art.

Each clutching one of John's thighs tightly, they buried the sides of their heads into his crotch and craned their necks upwards, straining towards the thick, rigid shaft of his prick. Two pink tongues snaked out, delivering slow, lapping, upward strokes to either side of the throbbing column of flesh, making it dance and twitch violently.

John was in seventh heaven as the two girls avidly licked

his cock, their hair tickling the sensitive insides of his thigh in a sensual manner. He had been at the Paradise Club less than an hour, yet already the sexual delights he had been promised were being delivered. His brain swam with wild thoughts of the pleasures yet to come, and the knowledge that he had three whole weeks in which everything was possible. He remembered reading somewhere of a primitive pagan cult in which one young man of the tribe was selected each year to be the symbol of fertility. For twelve months, he would be treated like a god, hand-fed the finest food and fruits, expected to make love to every virgin and cossetted in every way humanly possible. At the end of his reign, of course, he would be put to death on the sacrificial altar – but no doubt died a happy man.

John wasn't too keen on the last part, but could only hope that Amanda and her companions were slightly more civilised. For the moment, he concentrated his efforts upon being a fertility god and enjoying himself.

The two girls had licked and kissed every inch of his stiff shaft now, and were rising on their knees to reach the top of the towering column. John shuddered with pleasure as their two hot tongues slavered over the sensitive head of his cock, priming the swollen dome to bursting point. As they licked, both girls stroked the pulsing shaft, running their slim, cool fingers up and down the engorged weapon with sensual, loving caresses.

Both Sam and Melanie had passed the point at which they were just putting on an act for the cameras. As she ran her fingers up and down John's gently pulsing rod, Melanie felt a sense of awe, marvelling at the stiffness and raw animal appeal of such a superb piece of manhood. Never in her life could she remember encountering a cock which would not fit completely within her grasp, for even squeezing tightly, she was unable to close her fingers completely around the distended shaft. Aware of the moist warmth of her flowing juices dribbling down the insides of her thighs, she wondered how it would feel to have such a throbbing beast inside her.

Sam's thoughts were more practical. She was concerned not with how it *might* feel, but when she was going to feel it, for she had already made up her mind to impale herself upon the mighty, meaty spike as soon as possible. Such was her single-minded determination towards this end, the presence of the cameras and an audience hardly mattered – although she found herself increasingly resentful of Melanie's presence. John's cock was a pleasure she did not really want to share, Sam thought, racking her brains for ways in which she might get rid of her rival. Failing to come up with any cunning subterfuge, she decided on direct, and desperate, action.

Still slavishly licking the bulging helmet, Sam squinted down the shaft of John's cock to where Melanie's hand played up and down the thickest part of the stalk, her fingers tracing out the throbbing, knobbly veins which pulsed beneath the outer skin. Sliding her own hand down over Melanie's knuckles, Sam raked her sharp nails across the back of the girl's hand.

Melanie shrieked in pain, snatching her hand away from John's cock as though she had been bitten by a snake. Snarling with rage, she turned her attention upon her assailant, clawing out towards the side of Sam's face.

Having initiated the attack, Sam was prepared for retaliation. As Melanie's hand flew towards her cheek, she seized the girl's wrist, twisting it violently.

Melanie screamed again, falling over onto her back and glaring up at Sam with blazing eyes. 'You bitch,' she spat angrily, rolling away in a smooth and graceful movement before coming to a rising crouch on her hands and knees, hissing like a big cat about to pounce.

The fight was on, Sam thought, eyeing her enraged partner and trying to work out her next move. Instinctively, she moved into a defensive position, moving away from John and rearing up on her knees, her hands outstretched and her fingers extended.

Events had moved so quickly that Miles was taken completely by surprise. He wasn't sure what had happened between the two girls, or quite what was happening now – but it looked like it could provide some spectacular footage. He jumped up and down in excited glee, yelling at the two cameramen. 'Keep filming, get everything. This could be dynamite.'

He continued to watch, fascinated, as the two girls clashed, hands clawing, legs kicking, breasts leaping. Then they were rolling over on the floor, nude and howling, their legs scissoring, open-mouthed cunts kissing in an erotic cat-fight.

John, totally bemused by the turn events had taken, backed away uncertainly, his hands crossed protectively over his rigid prick. He was hardly in a position to get involved, he figured, falling back to a position of comparative safety behind the nearest camera.

Too late, he realised that he had stepped out of the frying pan and into the fire. Sam and Melanie's battle seemed to have triggered off a wave of blood-lust amongst the female spectators, who were all already screaming out words of encouragement or insult to one or other of the contestants.

John's retreat behind the cameras put him firmly in their territory, making him at once a prize of war. Bella made a grab for him first, lunging forward to get her greedy hands on his towering totem.

Her attempt was greeted with howls of mob fury, as every other woman in the room except Shelley and Sally declared herself a combatant. Bella ended up flat on her back on the floor, with a high-heeled shoe pressed firmly across her throat. There was a brief flurry of other bodies before Freda emerged triumphant, decimating the opposition with a succession of high kicks and karate blows. Screaming out a blood-chilling war-cry which would have struck terror into even her wild Nordic ancestors, the blonde Amazon brought John crashing to the floor in a flying rugby tackle and promptly leapt upon her prize. Seating herself astride his belly, facing his feet, she wrenched his proud cock from his protective grasp and wrapped her arms around it, holding it tightly against her belly. The trophy thus claimed and won, she glared up at the other women with open hostility in her ice-blue eyes, daring any challenge to her warrior supremacy.

There were no takers. Everyone present had encountered the formidable Freda before, if only on the massage table – and there was no percentage in taking on a young woman whose selection of party tricks included cracking walnuts between her shoulderblades. A deathly silence fell over the gymnasium as Freda slowly and majestically rose to her feet, locked a powerful arm firmly around John's waist and half-dragged, half-carried him away to her private sanctum.

Miles finally managed to separate the struggling Sam and Melanie, holding them bodily apart long enough for tempers to cool down. He looked up just in time to see John's naked rump disappearing through the emergency fire doors at the far end of the gymnasium. With a weary, resigned sigh, he ordered the cameras to stop rolling and turned to Amanda for consolation, draping his arm over her shoulder.

'At a rough guess, I'd say that was the end of filming for the day,' he observed philosophically. 'What say we adjourn to the bar and you fix me a good stiff drink?'

Amanda's eyes twinkled mischievously. Seeing John's stupendous cock again had made her feel incredibly horny. Deprived of the genuine article, Miles appeared to be the nearest, and the next best thing. 'I've got a better idea,' she murmured sexily. 'Why don't we adjourn to my room instead and I'll fix you a good stiff prick?'

Miles was taken somewhat aback, and secretly rather flattered at Amanda's sudden interest. In the face of such an attractive offer, it didn't occur to him to question the reason why. Had he done so, perhaps his ego might have taken a slight battering, but for now he was quite content to take what a benign fate was throwing in his path.

Grinning happily, he dropped his arm to Amanda's slim waist and hugged her enthusiastically. 'Tell you what – we'll compromise,' he told her. 'We'll adjourn to *my* room and have both. I've got half a bottle of Scotch and a full ice-bucket.'

Amanda wasn't disposed to argue. She shrugged her

aquiescence. 'So what are we doing?' she queried. 'Celebrating, or drowning our sorrows?'

'Celebrating, definitely,' Miles said firmly. 'Tomorrow we start making our movie with the hottest new male lead since Valentino.'

Amanda's eyes twinkled. 'I take it you're pleased with our John, then?'

Miles grinned. 'Pleased? I'm bloody delighted,' he said fervently. 'The man's a marvel.'

Amanda giggled. 'Every inch a star, would you say?'

Miles nodded, appreciating the joke. 'They don't come any inchier,' he shot back, grinning.

Chapter Fifteen

Amanda's lush body was everything Miles had dared to imagine – and then some. Naked, his second tumbler of Scotch in his hand, he lay on the bed with his back propped against the pillows as she paraded herself unashamedly in front of him.

Devouring every curve with the air of a connoisseur, Miles savoured the full, rounded softness of her delicious breasts, imagining the sweet taste of her cherry-like nipples between his lips. Travelling down her flat belly, his eyes took in her slim waist, the gorgeous flare of her hips and her long, slender legs. Returning upwards again, he smiled inwardly at the rare sight of a truly natural blonde, evidenced by the little triangle of golden curls which adorned the cleft between her legs.

'Beautiful,' he breathed, huskily. He placed his glass down on the bedside table, stretching out his hand towards her. 'Come over here. I want to feel you, see if you're real.'

It was not so much the compliment as the way in which it was delivered. Just as at their first meeting, Amanda sensed that Miles really liked women. She felt a vague thrill of pleasure run through her body, and a rush of strange yet oddly familiar emotions through her mind. She could hardly remember how long it had been since a man had affected her in this way. Miles had told her she was beautiful – and suddenly Amanda *felt* beautiful. There was a gentleness, a sincerity about him – even though it was patently obvious that his charm had been well-practised.

She stepped towards the bed, standing over him. Reaching up, Miles cupped his hands under the swelling softness of her firm young breasts, running his thumbs lightly over her nipples.

He smiled, nodding to himself. 'Oh yes, you're real alright,' he murmured. He ran his fingers down the plane of her belly, marvelling at the silky smoothness of her flawless skin.

'You look pretty real yourself,' Amanda pointed out, glancing down at his rapidly stiffening prick. Reaching down and taking it in her hand, she ran her fingers up and down the swelling shaft, shivering with pleasure as it jerked and twitched at her touch. Tightening her grip, she squeezed it gently, feeling the faint, spasmodic throb of pulsing blood which coursed along the bulging underside. All thoughts of John's monster prick were gone now, as though it, or he, had never existed. Amanda felt light-headed, almost as if she were drugged or dreaming. She had the strangest feeling that the present moment had been waiting to happen for most of her adult life, that it had somehow been pre-destined that she and Miles would eventually end up making love together.

Still holding his cock, she sank down onto the bed beside him, resting her blonde head against his chest. Miles kissed her hair, in a surprisingly gentle and innocent gesture, reaching up to stroke the side of her cheek.

Amanda found it quite moving, and even a little frightening. 'This wasn't quite what I was expecting,' she murmured, needing to share something of her feelings with him.

Miles nodded, tracing the delicate shape of her soft lips with his fingertips. 'Yes, I know,' he said quietly. 'Exciting, isn't it?'

It was a perfect choice of word, Amanda thought, suddenly understanding her own feelings a little better. It wasn't a sense of fear at all that she was experiencing. It was the thrill of anticipation.

She reached for his hand, still stroking her face. Sliding it over her breasts and down her belly, she pressed it between her thighs, tucking his fingers into the hot, moist cleft between her labial lips.

It was an open invitation which Miles was not going to resist. Slowly, he slid two fingers into Amanda's juicy wetness and began to explore the hot, slippery walls of her cunt.

Amanda sighed, relaxing and enjoying the feeling of gentle penetration. Using the heel of his hand, Miles massaged the soft lips of her cunt with a slow, circular motion, adding to the pleasure. She continued to hold his stiff cock, toying with it, occasionally giving it a gentle squeeze or tickling his balls with her fingernails.

Several dreamy, contented minutes passed, in which they were both perfectly happy to gently pleasure each other in this fashion. Holding back at the point of simple eroticism, rather than actual stimulation, neither was aware of the undercurrent of passion which built up slowly all around them like the lull before a storm.

When it finally broke, it did so with a suddenness and a ferocity which surprised them both. One second Miles was lolling contentedly against the soft pillows, and the next he was throwing himself over Amanda's body, pressing her down into the heaving water mattress and feverishly kissing and biting at her neck and shoulders.

Amanda responded immediately, as the full power of their mutual attraction was suddenly released. Her body stiffened, her pelvic muscles thrusting violently up against the crushing weight of his body. The sudden explosion of passion lent her extra strength, knocking him onto his back. Following through in an unbroken, fluid movement, Amanda clambered on top of him and ground her belly down against the hardness of his cock.

The feeling inflamed her even more, sending a savage jolt of pure lust coursing through her belly. She brought up her knees, rising to a crouch and straddling Miles' thighs. Wriggling into position, she took hold of his stiff cock and guided it to the wet lips of her slit, pressing the bulbous head into the damp crease. With a forward thrust of her pelvic muscles, Amanda slid herself onto its throbbing length with a throaty grunt of satisfaction.

Sighing deeply as the thick shaft moved along her well-lubricated tunnel, Amanda spread her knees wider and rolled her arse around to ease its passage all the way up to the neck of her womb. Knowing that she could take no more, she threw herself down on his chest and clamped her mouth over his in a searing, fiery kiss.

Miles threw his arms around her back, his fingers clawing into the firm flesh of her buttocks. Pulling at her, he rocked her up and down upon his imprisoned prick, humping his own arse up from the bed as he did so.

The pulsing rod filled every inch of Amanda's cunt, vibrating against the soft and slippery inner walls. She clenched her internal muscles, sucking at it and squeezing it inside her until Miles groaned with pleasure.

He let his arse flop back on the bed, lying there quiescent for a few moments while she milked his cock with consummate precision and artistry. Then, grunting with exertion, he reversed their positions yet again, rolling Amanda over onto her back. He lifted her legs, slipping them over his shoulders either side of his neck and hunching forward until she was almost bent double. Pumping his hips, he thrust into her with such speed and force that Amanda could feel the weight of his balls slapping against the cheeks of her arse.

From the way Miles was grunting, Amanda figured he would come fairly quickly, and she didn't want to be left behind. Concentrating her senses upon the feel of his thick cock reaming the inside of her cunt, she tuned in to her own body, willing it to reach that first plateau which invariably preceded her own orgasm. It began almost at once, with little rippling waves of pleasure starting out in the pit of her belly and spreading luxuriantly out to all other parts of her body. Her thighs and belly were suffused with a warm glow, and she could feel the prickling of moist heat within her cunt as her juices began to flow more heavily.

But it seemed she had underestimated Miles' stamina and sexual technique. Just when she thought that he must explode at any second, he suddenly stopped ramming into her and pulled back until the blunt head of his cock was poised between her wet cunt lips. He looked down at her, a wide grin on his face.

'Fancy a little change of tempo?' he enquired, cockily.

Before Amanda could answer, he withdrew completely and leapt off the bed, showing remarkable reserves of stamina for a man who had just been humping away like a demon. Bending down again, he grasped Amanda by the shoulders and pulled her to her feet, turning her round and positioning her until she faced the bed, about three feet from the edge. Gently, but firmly, he urged her to bend over, placing the flat of her hands on the bed so that her pert little arse reared provocatively in the air.

Standing himself behind her, Miles eased her feet apart until he was completely satisfied with her positioning, then fondled her arse lovingly. Taking a smoothly rounded cheek in either hand, he pulled them apart to reveal the open and inviting mouth of her brimming honeypot.

Amanda felt the thick head of his cock dancing between her legs for a few seconds and then it docked itself in her hot slit with the precision of a lunar landing module. A single gentle shove of his hips, and Miles was inside her again, the full length of his beautiful prick gliding up her well-oiled shaft like a hot piston-rod.

Amanda groaned softly at the feeling of total penetration, wriggling her arse deliciously to spread the sensation to every part of her pleasure-hungry love canal. Despite the temporary break in their love-making, she was still primed for orgasm, and the fluttery little spasms of pleasure deep in her belly started up again almost immediately.

As if sensing this, Miles slowed down the pace and intensity of his thrusts, moving his hips in a gentle, regular rhythm. His cock soared in and out of her dripping cunt with long, graceful strokes, sending quivering vibrations of pleasure all the way from her clitoris to her cervix. Bending over her back, he reached under her armpits and scooped up her soft, dangling breasts in his hands, cupping them gently and rolling the erect nipples around with his fingertips.

Amanda let out a long, low, shuddering sigh as this final stimulation tripped her into the first stages of primary orgasm. She rode the sensation for all it was worth, enjoying herself like a child on a theme park roller-coaster. His prick was sloshing loosely inside her now, a sudden flood of lubrication dampening out the sensation of penetration and friction for both of them. Amanda responded by closing her legs and thighs together, tensing her stomach muscles to tighten her cunt around Miles' cock.

The move was obviously appreciated. Miles let out a little grunt of satisfaction. 'Oh, yes – that's better.' He thrust into her more forcefully, his belly making little smacking sounds as it slapped against her wet buttocks.

Amanda began to shudder as the second wave of orgasm rolled up behind the first. Gathering power, it rose in her belly like a huge ocean wave, curling towards its final release upon the shore.

'Faster,' she urged Miles, wanting desperately to carry him along on the wave's crest.

He redoubled his efforts, spurred on to a second wind by the heady aroma of Amanda's flowing love-juice and the feeling of tightness and pressure in his own loins. Pumping away furiously, he built up his rhythm to a crescendo, his arse moving in a blur of white flesh.

Amanda's orgasm broke suddenly, with a violence which

surprised them both. Every muscle in her body seemed to clench and tighten, a feeling of fiery heat burning deep into her very bones. With a scream which suggested agony rather than ecstasy, she let herself be swept up in the flood, hardly aware of Miles spurting his own contribution into her overflowing fanny.

Amanda collapsed onto the bed, sprawling out on her back as Miles sank down beside her. Breathing heavily, they lay together without speaking for several minutes. It was Miles who finally broke the silence. His voice was awkward, a little stilted.

'Look, Amanda – there's something I want to say to you, only I don't want you to get the wrong idea,' he started hesitantly.

Not quite sure what was coming, Amanda was equally guarded as she answered. 'So try me,' she suggested.

There was a thoughtful pause as Miles tried to frame his thoughts and words. 'Look, that was really great,' he said finally. 'Only I don't want you to get it out of context, if you know what I mean.'

Amanda wasn't sure she did know what he meant, but she had a sneaking suspicion that Miles was somehow skirting round the old 'I enjoyed fucking you but I don't want to get involved' routine.

She turned on her side to face him, smiling easily.

'Maybe it's you who's getting things out of context,' she told him. 'I'm a big girl, Miles. Believe it or not, I can enjoy a session of good old simple sex without imagining I'm madly and passionately in love.'

Miles looked aggrieved. 'That wasn't what I was trying to say,' he muttered.

Amanda felt rather foolish. She had obviously got hold of the wrong end of the stick, and hurt his feelings into the bargain.

'Sorry,' she apologised. 'So what was it you meant?'

Miles sighed. 'What I was trying to explain was that what just happened was terrific, but it was between us – just you and me,' he said.

Amanda was getting a little confused. 'Well I did gather that,' she pointed out. 'I mean, we haven't just taken part in a thousand-person orgy or anything.'

Miles looked even more awkward, aware that he wasn't explaining himself very well at all. He gave it one more try.

'Look, what I'm trying to say is that I don't want you to confuse what just happened between us with anything else,' he said finally. 'Not with our professional arrangement as partners in the film, or with the film itself. In a nutshell, I don't want you getting caught up in this movie business. People sometimes do, because I've seen it before, and I don't want it happening to you.'

At last, Amanda thought she was beginning to understand, and found it rather flattering. She felt a wave of affection for the man, reaching out to clasp his hand.

'Miles, I do believe you're trying to be chivalrous,' she exclaimed. 'You're trying to protect me from the big bad world of dirty movies.'

He nodded awkwardly. 'Something like that,' he admitted. 'It's just that I have to be on my toes all the time to keep two different worlds apart, stop them from blurring into one another. Sex is sex, and pornography is pornography. I want you to know where you belong in relationship to me.'

Amanda gave him a warm, understanding smile. 'I think

I've got the picture, Miles – and thank you,' she told him gently. She was thoughtful for a while. 'And how does Shelley fit into all this?' she asked finally, curious.

Miles shrugged. 'Shelley is an example of what I was trying to point out. She just wants to screw her way into the movies,' he said bluntly. 'And she's as conscious of that as I am.'

Amanda patted his hand. 'Relax, Miles. I have absolutely no ambitions to become a second Linda Lovelace,' she told him.

'Well, just as long as you understand,' Miles said, feeling that he had made his point at last. 'It can be a pernicious business, sucking people in, letting them become involved before they really know what's happening. Then, suddenly, they find themselves swept up into a world where sex and pornography become indistinguishable from one another. A world of blind, mindless fucking where one body becomes much like another, and individuals don't matter. Films aren't *real*, you see – any more than the characters in them are real. And perhaps even the people connected with them aren't real either.'

Miles fell silent then, giving Amanda a lot of food for thought. It was a sobering, but caring little speech, and she appreciated his concern. It would probably have been un-necessarily hurtful to him to point out that three years in the Paradise Club might already have had much the same effect.

Chapter Sixteen

Shelley was in a jubilant mood the following morning, ready and eager for the first day of shooting. She was on set a good half-hour before any of the crew appeared, pacing the gymnasium floor fretfully as she waited for everyone else to arrive and take up their positions.

The girl seemed really hyped up, Amanda thought, wondering if she had perhaps popped a few uppers. Partly out of curiosity, and partly because one of the few ground rules in the Paradise Club was no drugs on the premises, she managed to get close enough to the girl to take a careful look at her eyes. They were bright and sparkling with enthusiasm, but showed no signs of being unduly dilated.

She was probably just excited, Amanda decided – although whether she was looking forward to the sex scenes themselves or the fame they were going to bring her was anyone's guess. Most likely a bit of both, Amanda thought.

By ten o'clock, everything looked more or less set up. The cameramen were in position, Franklin had created an effective bedroom set and was now busying himself sorting out the minimal wardrobe requirements. Emily had finally been persuaded to come out of her room and wandered about like a love-sick puppy, casting her eyes around hopefully for a glimpse of Sally.

Shelley was slightly disappointed when the newly-named Dirk Scabbard turned up instead of John, but consoled herself with the news that she wouldn't have to share this particular shooting session with any other females.

Franklin fussed around them like a mother hen, looking jumpy and excited as Dirk stripped down to his underpants. Virtually ignoring Shelley, he thrust a small bundle into her hands. 'Your costume,' he muttered, his eyes firmly fixed on the bulging crotch of Dirk's Y-fronts.

Shelley looked over at Miles, surprise showing on her face. 'Costume, Miles?' she queried. 'I thought the point of this film was to get undressed, not dress up.'

Miles smiled indulgently. 'You've got to have something on to start with,' he pointed out. 'You'll take it off again when things get started, of course.'

Shelley looked down at the small bundle in her hand. Her fingers had already encountered and recognised the soft, shiny feel of leather – but the actual nature and purpose of the skimpy garment were not immediately apparent to the eye. Curious, she unfolded what there was of the costume and tried to work out what it was. It appeared to be a diminutive G-string attached to half a dozen straps in no particular order.

Miles noticed her examining the garment with a baffled expression and hurried over, smiling helpfully.

'Here, I'll show you how it goes on,' he offered, steering her away towards a corner of the gym which had been curtained off as a changing area.

Safely inside, Shelley stripped down to the buff and examined the black leather gear again, still unable to fathom out how it could possibly serve as a costume.

Miles grinned, taking it from her hands. He bent down and guided Shelley's feet between two of the straps. Gathering up the other four, he pulled them up, helped Shelley to lock them into position under her crotch and settled the G-string over her pubic mound.

The remaining straps had heavy chrome buckles on them. Miles unclipped a couple of these and gestured for Shelley to lift her arms in the air. As she obliged, he slipped the remaining straps around her torso and pulled them tightly into position.

'There,' he murmured triumphantly. 'You're all kitted up.'

Shelley was aware of a vague discomfort around her breasts. Looking down on the weird garment, she could see why. The straps around her thighs were pulled tight, making the flesh bulge out suggestively. The straps then went round to lift up her buttocks, squeezing them together into a sort of rear-end cleavage. The four top straps criss-crossed over her belly to encase her breasts tightly between thin strips of leather so that they looked as though they were peering out from behind iron bars. The whole ensemble was obviously designed to appeal to leather kinks and bondage freaks, but was most certainly not a turn-on for the wearer.

'Too tight?' Miles muttered with concern, noticing the look of anguish on Shelley's face.

The girl put on a brave face, reflecting that stardom was rarely achieved without sacrifice. 'I'll live,' she grunted. 'As long as I can manage to give up breathing for the next few minutes.'

'It won't be for long,' Miles assured her. 'Now, when you go on set, just march about looking very butch for a while – and make sure you give the cameras plenty of rear view stuff. Try to wiggle your arse around as much as you can.'

The instructions seemed fairly basic and undemanding, Shelley thought. Not exactly Royal Shakespeare Company material, but a nice easy introduction to thespian art.

'And what will our friend Dirk be doing while I'm wiggling my arse?' she wanted to know.

There was a slightly sheepish grin on Miles' face. 'Believe it or not, he'll be stripping off a long blonde wig, a padded bra, a lurex dress and a pair of frilly panties,' he told her.

Shelley gaped at him in astonishment. 'You're kidding.'

Miles shook his head. 'No, seriously – the punters really find this transvestite kick erotic, trust me. When Dirk first comes onto the set, everyone thinks he's another woman, so they get all fired up for some lesbian stuff. Then, when he strips off and reveals a hard-on, it comes as a surprise.'

Shelley looked extremely dubious. 'It'll be a bloody surprise to me if he has a hard-on after being dressed up in full drag,' she said cynically.

Miles shrugged. 'Yes, well, we might have to cut and fake it up a bit at that stage,' he admitted. 'But don't you worry about that now. Just leave it to me.'

'And after that?' Shelley demanded.

'After that we'll run straight into some bondage and dominatrix stuff. Then you can get out of your costume and get right down to some good old-fashioned humping.'

The end part sounded better, Shelley thought – although she wasn't too sure about the bit in the middle.

'This bondage and dominatrix stuff – is that whips and chains and all that sort of gear?' she queried.

'If you like,' Miles offered generously. 'Only try not to leave any ugly red weals. They don't look too good on camera.' He paused, eyeing her thoughtfully. 'So, got everything? Are we ready to roll?'

There was just one last thing which Shelley wasn't too sure about. 'Is there any set routine?' she wanted to know.

Miles thought for a second, then shook his head. 'No, not really. Just as long as we get a few minutes of each variation, I can put it all together in the cutting room later. Just do whatever comes to you – but don't forget to wiggle your arse about.'

Shelley nodded. 'I'll wiggle,' she promised. 'And then how about a bit of screaming and shouting when we come to the actual sex scene?'

Although it was said as a joke, Miles actually thought about the suggestion carefully for several seconds, finally shaking his head. 'Hmmm – nice little touch that,' he murmured aloud. 'But probably a bit over-dramatic for our audience.'

He stepped over to the curtain, pulling it back. 'OK, lights up,' he called out to Charlie. He returned to Shelley as the man pulled the switch, flooding the gymnasium with light. Patting her playfully on the rump, Miles urged her forward. 'Right – get out there and be a star,' he told her, following her through the curtains and heading over to join Amanda.

Shelley marched purposefully across the gymnasium floor

and onto the brilliantly-lit set . . . where she promptly froze! Struck with the complete paralysis of stage fright, she could only stand like a statue and gape glassy-eyed towards the cameras. There was a long and complete silence.

'Do something, you stupid bitch,' Franklin eventually piped out cattily. 'Even if it's only to shake your tits about.'

The jibe struck home, jolting Shelley out of her trance-like state. Her eyes blazing with anger, she stared out across the gym, trying to identify her persecutor. It was impossible to pick out individuals through the blinding glare of the bright lights. Addressing herself to little more than a pink blur, she spat back her reply.

'I'll bloody well shake you, you soggy little faggot,' she said furiously.

Franklin's little squeal of indignation was drowned out by the chorus of guffaws from the rest of the film crew. The laughter helped Shelley, somehow putting the whole thing into perspective. Her anger had broken her paralysis, and the warmth of humour washed away the last traces of stage fright. She looked out through the glare of the lights again, feeling comfortably insulated, safe in a little world of her own. Somehow, an irrational little feeling in the back of her mind told her if she couldn't see the audience then they couldn't see her either. It was only a film, she told herself – and films aren't real.

Remembering Miles' exhortations to wiggle her arse about, she began strutting about on the small set, poking her lovely posterior in the vague direction of the cameras. She wiggled, she shimmied, she shook her leather-encased body in every sexy and provocative way she could think of. Pretty soon, she was starting to enjoy herself.

Carried away, she hardly noticed when Dirk made his way onto the set, all togged up in his preposterous drag costume. Still bumping and grinding for all she was worth, Shelley continued to hog the cameras and the limelight.

'Come on then – move over so I can do my bit,' Dirk hissed at her. 'Who the hell do you think you are – Sarah bloody Bernhardt?' He moved into centre stage, preparing to go into his own strip routine.

Somewhat reluctantly, Shelley edged out of camera shot towards the big double bed which dominated the small set. Waiting impatiently, she watched Dirk as he began to take off the lurex dress, revealing the cleverly-padded bra and fake flesh-coloured plastic cleavage beneath it. Finally down to the blonde wig and his underpants, Dirk prepared to reveal his manhood to the cameras. The wig went first, then he hooked his thumbs into the elasticated waistband of the pants.

She had been right about the erection – or rather the lack of one Shelley thought as Dirk's Y-fronts dropped to the floor. After all the build-up, the sight of his limp and dangling prick was something of an anti-climax.

'Cut,' Miles shouted, and the bright studio lights snapped off abruptly. He strode across towards the set, looking remarkably cheerful under the circumstances.

'That was great,' he told Shelley enthusiastically. 'You had me worried there for a second, but when you came through, you really came through.'

Shelley bathed in the praise for a moment, then nodded down at Dirk's flaccid appendage. 'Which is more than you can say for Danny La Rue here,' she muttered sarcastically. 'So what do we do now?'

Miles tapped the side of his nose. 'Now we make a bit of movie magic,' he said confidently. 'Remember that old saying – the camera never lies?'

Shelley nodded. 'Of course I've heard it,' she admitted. 'So what of it?'

Miles grinned hugely. 'It's total bullshit,' he announced. 'The camera lies all the bloody time. If it didn't, there wouldn't even be a movie business.'

He turned his attention to Dirk, who was standing there looking rather foolish and embarrassed. 'Right – this is where you learn the hardest part of being a stud in dirty movies,' he announced. 'Get it up.'

Dirk looked at him dumbly. 'What?'

'You heard me – get it up,' Miles repeated, nodding at the young man's limp cock. 'If you can't get an instant erection to order, then you haven't got much of a future in this business.'

'Would you like a bit of help, sweetie?' Franklin offered.

Dirk shot him a scathing look. He glanced over at Shelley before returning his attention to Miles with a silent request in his eyes.

By way of an answer, Miles shook his head slowly. 'This one's cold turkey, I'm afraid,' he said sympathetically. 'It's something you have to do for yourself or you might as well pack your suitcase and go home.'

Finally accepting that he wasn't going to get any artificial help, Dirk stared down at his dangling cock, willing it to rise to the occasion. His forehead creased into a frown of rapt concentration as he desperately tried to think of every erotic image he could conjure up in his mind, starting with his current girl-friend Sandra.

Attractive as she was, and serviceable enough in bed, Sandra failed to bring about the required response. Dirk turned his attention to popular movie actresses, dreaming of a long line of screen sirens queueing up to suck his cock. This achieved only limited success. His limp cock jerked sluggishly a couple of times, inflated to semi-hard, but refused to stiffen into full erection.

What he needed was something a bit more direct, less fanciful, Dirk thought. He turned his attention to the more accessible Shelley, concentrating his gaze on the creamy white flesh of her swelling tits straining against the black leather straps of her costume.

The trouble was, he really wasn't into the leather or bondage kick, Dirk realised regretfully. He took his sex more or less straight – although he did appreciate a really decent blow-job. His eyes travelled to Shelley's generous mouth, the ripe softness of her lips.

A good cock-sucking mouth, he realised. Full, red lips which looked as though they could caress a stiff cock softly, yet be firm enough to apply gentle, sensuous pressure. It was easy to imagine them gliding wetly up and down the length of his throbbing prick, while her tongue flickered teasingly around its swollen head. The image grew and intensified. In his mind's eye, Dirk saw Shelley's blonde head bobbing furiously up and down between his parted thighs, her cheeks bulging as his cock filled her mouth and throat.

'That's my boy,' Miles called out jubilantly. 'I knew you could do it.'

Jolted out of his erotic daydream, Dirk looked down at his prick again, and was almost surprised to see that it had sprung into throbbing stiffness, sticking out like a miniature flagpole and jerking faintly up and down.

'Now, put your pants back on, wait until I say "action" and then peel them off again,' Miles instructed. 'Then go straight into the business with Shelley. By the time we've cut and spliced the film, nobody is going to know you didn't have a raging hard-on in the first place.'

Delighted that he appeared to have passed his first dramatic test, Dirk did as he was told. Miles ordered the studio lights back on, the cameras rolling, and filming resumed.

Shelley had decided on a bit of spanking rather than resorting to instruments of flagellation. Pulling Dirk onto the bed, she laid him out across her lap and began to smack his rounded buttocks with the flat of her hand. Dirk yelped with genuine pain, since the girl was putting her heart and soul into her role and the blows really stung. The cheeks of his arse quickly turned bright pink and then a flaming red as Shelley kept up the punishment. Gritting his teeth, Dirk wondered how long the torture would last, since the bloody girl seemed to be really enjoying herself.

Eventually, it was the heat of the studio lights which came to his rescue. Her arms were tired and she was starting to perspire heavily from the exertion. Shelley began to worry about her make-up running and brought the spanking session to an end. She pushed Dirk off her lap, rolling him over onto his back, noting with some relief that he had managed to keep his erection. Admiring the stiff weapon, she had to admit to herself that it really wasn't a bad cock at all, as cocks went. If not exactly a thrill machine, it looked more than capable of delivering some degree of pleasure. Perhaps more to the point, it represented the chance to get out of her tight and uncomfortable costume, which would be a pleasure in itself.

Shelley set about doing exactly this, unhooking the black straps and discarding the leather contraption with a sense of relief. Naked again, she turned her attention back to Dirk's quivering prick, wondering what to do with it first.

Mindful that she was performing for the cameras rather than for her own pleasure, Shelley decided not to suck Dirk's cock, even though it did look rather tasty. After the spanking, she had been surprised to find that he still had a hard-on at all, and something told her that it might be only a fragile one. A blow-job could well trip the man over the edge, and Miles would not be too pleased if she brought Dirk off too soon and buggered up further filming until he could get it back up again.

She decided to ride him horse-back style instead. That would give the cameras some nice views of her arse and cunt, and they could zoom in for some graphic close-ups of Dirk's glistening cock as it slid in and out of her.

Wasting no time now that she had made up her mind, Shelley threw herself astride the recumbent Dirk and took his stiff love-machine in her hand, guiding it towards the hairy lips of her slit. Plugging the blunt head into the mouth of her hole and sticking out her arse for the cameras, Shelley allowed herself to sink onto the engorged shaft in a slow and exaggerated fashion.

Dirk let out a throaty moan as Shelley's tight but slippery cunt engulfed his pulsating manhood. He jerked his hips, thrusting his pelvis upward to meet her as she bore down on to his belly. Rising on her knees, Shelley backed off, acutely conscious of the fact that all the cameras wanted to see was as much cock and cunt as possible. She raised herself until the mouth of her fanny just held the domed helmet of his prick in a loose grip, then began rolling her arse around in a slow, lazy, figure-of-eight pattern.

The exquisite sensation of having the sensitive tip of his cock thus caressed by Shelley's moist labial lips made Dirk shudder with pleasure. He abandoned any further attempts to thrust upwards. Grunting contentedly, he lay back passively to enjoy the benefits of the girl's unique and highly stimulating technique.

Feeling him relax beneath her, Shelley knew that she was now in total and utter control. Flexing her knees, she added a slight up and down movement to her pelvic gyrations so that the first two or three inches of Dirk's cock slipped in and out of her wet hole like a slightly eccentric piston.

Dirk's grunts became gasps of pleasure as a new wave of sensation tore through his loins. He was unable to resist stabbing upwards, trying to cram more of his cock into this wonderful, wet love-shaft which was capable of delivering such erotic delights.

Sensing that he was close to coming, Shelley eased up on the figure-of-eight movement, but it was already too late. Dirk's jerky upward thrusts became savage, desperate lunges now, as he strove to ram the full length of his prick deep into her delectable cunt. He bucked his hips furiously, knowing only the pure animal urge of raw sex and its solitary purpose – to spurt his hot seed into the fecund ripeness of the woman's womb.

Like triggered like. Shelley's body responded to the sudden upsurge of masculine power automatically, releasing her own lust. Completely ignoring the requirements of the cameras now, she threw herself down on Dirk's slick tool and ground her pelvis against his. Sod the film, she thought. Sod Miles and sod the cameras. She had done enough for them. Now it was time to get something for herself. Dirk was about to shoot his load and she didn't intend to let him come on his own.

Riding her steed like a National Hunt jockey in sight of the winning post, she urged him first into a canter and then into a full-blooded gallop. Screaming jubilantly, she felt the hot spurt of Dirk's creamy ejaculation mere seconds before she too came.

With a savage grin on her face, Shelley turned her head to face Miles.

'And that, as I think you say in this business, is a wrap,' she announced triumphantly, before collapsing upon Dirk's sticky belly.

Chapter Seventeen

Miles seemed more than content with the day's filming as the crew prepared to wrap it up for the evening. Besides the scene with Shelley and Dirk, he had managed to shoot a few good outdoor sequences with Sam and Melanie for possible padding in the final cut, and John had more than justified his faith in him by performing faultlessly. Indeed, Miles was quite convinced that the man's massive prick would sell the finished film on its own merits, if only to a female audience.

He was particularly proud of the impromptu scene in which Sam, Melanie and Shelley had all subjected the stupendous organ to their oral ministrations. The sight of that towering column of stiff male flesh being lapped greedily by three tongues simultaneously was almost bound to become a porno movie classic, Miles felt.

News that shooting was coming to an end for the day had quickly filtered around the premises. With the set no longer closed to visitors, most of the female population of the club had drifted back into the gymnasium, either to catch a glimpse of the closing action or to lay claim to the male members of the cast and crew.

With her usual aggression, Freda had already collared

Wayne and Charlie and was guarding them as jealously as a male walrus with his harem of sea-cows. Sally was avidly eyeing up George the cameraman, whilst trying to ignore the lovesick glances which Emily threw in her direction at every possible opportunity.

Shelley had not been slow to notice the way in which Miles had been hovering around Amanda for most of the day, and was quite happy to write him off now that she had got what she wanted. Working on the basis of sticking to the tried and tested, she clung to Dirk possessively, reflecting that rising film stars ought to stick together. With Freda otherwise occupied, Sam and Melanie had booked John for the night, figuring that his cock must feel at least as good as it tasted. That left Derek, the handsome blond second cameraman for Bella – although she was becoming a trifle worried by the furtive little smiles he kept exchanging with Franklin. She was already half-tempted to try and throw her lot in with Sam and Melanie, figuring that one-third of a heterosexual man was better from her point of view than a whole homosexual.

Amanda felt quite flattered that Miles had obviously thrown over the undisputed sexual attraction of Shelley in her favour. She basked in his attention like an adolescent schoolgirl, clutching at his hand and smiling up at him frequently.

The gymnasium cleared gradually, Miles supervised the unloading of the day's film cans and entrusted them to Emily for safe storage. He turned his attention to Amanda, slipping one arm around her slim waist.

'Well, it looks as though most people have paired off for the night,' he observed. 'That Paradise magic you talked about seems to be working.'

Amanda chuckled. 'It never fails. The joint will be jumping tonight, as they say.' She grinned up at him. 'Pity you're not set up for night shooting. You could probably make three full-length movies before the morning.'

Miles shook his head, his eyes twinkling. 'No thanks. I've had enough film-making for one day. Besides, I was planning on getting a bit of that magic for myself.'

Amanda played coy. 'Oh, really?' she said. 'And did you have anyone in particular in mind?'

Miles went along with the little game. 'No, not really,' he said casually. 'I thought I'd just grab myself the first attractive woman who happened to be handy.'

Amanda glanced down at his arm around her waist, smiling broadly. 'Now isn't that a coincidence?' she murmured. 'I was planning to do exactly the same with the first good-looking man.'

'Looks like we're stuck with each other,' Miles said, pretending to frown. 'I suppose we'll just have to make the best of it.'

Amanda looked thoughtful. 'It certainly looks that way,' she agreed. 'The question is – shall we do anything about it?'

Miles shook his head slowly. 'Wrong question,' he muttered emphatically.

Amanda was thrown slightly. The game seemed to have changed. A look of concern crossed her face. 'So what's the right question?' she asked, slightly unsure of herself.

Miles grinned, hugging her tightly. 'Your room or mine?' he said, removing all doubts from Amanda's mind.

Amanda answered impulsively. 'Mine,' she said firmly. 'It's nearer.'

She locked her arm around his waist, relieved to realise that it had been a game after all. Just for a minute there, she had been really worried. Cuddling each other like a pair of teenage lovers, they danced towards the gymnasium doors.

They were both tense and expectant by the time they reached Amanda's private suite. A sense of urgency seemed to possess them both. Hardly over the threshold, they both stripped off their clothes hastily.

Miles patted Amanda's smooth and rounded arse playfully as he urged her towards the bed. He stood watching as she lay down, stretching herself luxuriously and exposing every inch of her lush body for his approval. He ran his eyes appreciatively over her superb figure, lingering on the gentle rise and fall of her superb breasts as she breathed deeply. Only when he had feasted himself to the point of gluttony did he sink down onto the bed beside her.

He rolled onto his side and pressed against her, letting his body melt into the warm glow of her soft flesh. Laying his hand on her smooth belly, he stroked it lovingly, his fingers exploring the smooth elasticity of her taut skin. Toying in the neat depression of her navel for a few seconds, his fingers moved on, creeping down through the silky triangle of her pubic hairs to the softness of her thighs and the gentle warmth between them.

Amanda spread her legs in response to his touch, allowing him free and unrestrained access to her most intimate parts. Miles rolled the ball of his hand over the faint hump of her pubic mound, his fingers straining through the soft cleft of her slit and seeking the damp little button of her clit.

Amanda moaned softly, anticipating the moment when his probing fingers would slip into the juicy recesses of her cunt. She was already hot and moist, feeling the warm prickling of her vaginal secretions as her love-tunnel prepared itself for penetration.

It did not come as quickly as she had been expecting. Lingering in the slippery nectar of her feminine secretions for a moment, Miles slid his fingers down through the silky slit of her cunt and into the tight cleft between the cheeks of her arse. Spreading his hand under her crotch, he gently inserted one finger into the puckered little orifice of her anus and rolled his thumb into her cunt.

Amanda quivered with pleasure at the sudden and unexpected thrill of this dual stimulation. She wriggled her arse, demanding more.

Miles got the message. Rotating his slippery finger gently, he drilled into her arsehole up to the knuckle, waggling his thumb from side to side at the same time. The ball of his hand was pressed tightly against Amanda's clitoris, and this added stimulation sent a shiver rippling through her groin. Reaching out, she slid her hand under his stiff cock, so that her fingers were cupped beneath his heavy balls and the thick shaft lay against her wrist.

She scratched at the leathery sac of his scrotum with a featherlight touch of her fingernails, causing Miles to let out a little grunt of pleasure. Pulling her hand back slightly, she felt the full fleshy thickness of his cock in her palm, and closed her fingers gently around it. The stiff rod jumped in her grip, the swollen head throbbing faintly against the inside of her wrist. Tightening her grip, Amanda squeezed the base of Miles' cock, slowly rubbing the loose skin up and down against the steel-like shaft within.

They lay together in this way for nearly a quarter of an hour, each delivering gentle pleasure to the other. Miles continued to roll his thumb around in her flowing honeypot, making the juices spill out and run down to lubricate his finger sliding slowly in and out of her arsehole.

Finally, by unspoken mutual consent, it was time to travel further down the road to sensual pleasures. Miles pulled his finger out of Amanda's tight little arsehole, stroking her wet cunt with the flat of his palm as he withdrew his hand altogether. Amanda let his stiff cock slip out of her grasp as he pulled away from her and stood up briefly, before sinking back onto the bed beside her with his feet towards the pillows. Sensing what he wanted, Amanda wriggled onto her side and adjusted her body position until they were entwined in a classic *soixante-neuf*. Her tongue probed for the swollen head of his cock, licking the smooth dome briefly before lifting it clear of the bed so that she could slide her wet lips onto it. Mouthing it gently, Amanda grunted contentedly as Miles pressed his face between her thighs and began lapping at the hot, stiff little button of her clitoris with the end of his tongue.

Amanda opened her mouth to let out a deep sigh of satisfaction. At the very same instant, Miles felt his stomach muscles contract in an involuntary spasm of pleasure. The movement jerked his hips, sending the full length of his cock soaring into Amanda's open mouth. Making the most of the sudden and unexpected treat, she closed her lips upon the throbbing shaft quickly, sucking at it with the insides of her cheeks.

Miles groaned in ecstasy as he felt the whole length of his prick engulfed by Amanda's warm, wet mouth. Responding in kind, he nuzzled deeper into her crotch, spreading her fleshy labial lips apart with his nose and mouth and sliding his tongue deep into her slippery shaft until it would stretch no more. Each of them thrust hungrily against the other, pressing face to crotch, crotch to face with the tickling feel of pubic hair against their lips. It was a moment of total intimacy which could not last. Before Miles could be smothered to death, or Amanda choked, they pulled apart reluctantly, each gasping desperately for breath.

'A hell of a way for a pair of lovers to commit mutual suicide,' Amanda observed, laughing. 'Beats the shit out of jumping off a cliff together, doesn't it?'

The brief moment of shared humour served as a natural break in their lovemaking. They rolled apart, Miles turning himself the right way up again so that they lay together on their backs, content merely to be together.

Both of them completely lost track of time. There seemed to be no hurry, no urgent need to consummate the feelings of sensuality which they shared. It was a good feeling, Amanda thought, realising that it had been a long time since she had felt so contented and relaxed with a man.

For his part, Miles found it strange, even slightly worrying. He stared at his still-quivering prick with detached fascination, wondering why he did not have the overpowering urge to ram it into the juicy cunt of the beautiful young woman beside him. Perhaps being back in the dirty movie business had exorcised all his animal lust out of him, he thought fancifully. Perhaps when you immersed yourself completely in raw sexual activity, it was like a glutton gorging himself. Totally stuffed and satiated on junk food, even the most delicious caviare lost its appeal.

Then Amanda wriggled against him so that their thighs touched. The gentle heat of her body surged into Miles' flesh, driving all such idle thoughts from his mind. Of course he wanted her, he told himself. Of course he hungered for the body of this gorgeous creature.

But it was a sudden wave of affection, rather than lust, which spurred him into action. He rolled over onto her flat belly, prising her legs apart with his knees.

Knowing that the time had come, Amanda reached for his prick, guiding it down between her hot thighs. Rising slightly on his knees, Miles allowed her to press the thick knob against the welcoming wetness of her cunt and then sank down again.

A feeling of total satisfaction washed over them both as his stiff shaft sank effortlessly into place. Miles let his cock glide down the slippery walls of her receptive sheath, sighing with delight as her very insides seemed to close around it, sucking at it with a thousand little mouths.

Amanda's legs came up around his buttocks, her feet locking firmly together in the small of his back. Miles groaned softly, rocking his hips gently from side to side as Amanda swallowed his manhood completely. It was as if his cock had just found where it truly belonged, he thought. As though his cock, and Amanda's cunt, were two parts of some perfect machine which had been designed as a precision fit, each one needing the other to make it work.

With a feeling of exhilaration, Miles began to make love in a way which he had almost forgotten.

Chapter Eighteen

Slow and gentle love-making was about the very last thing on Freda's mind at that moment. Having dragged Wayne and Charlie into her private sanctum and locked the massage room doors behind her, there was only pure lust in her heart. It had been a good few months since she had been lucky enough to get two pricks all to herself, and she was determined to enjoy them both to the full.

The two men exchanged a knowing, dirty wink as she stripped off in front of them. If ever a woman had been designed to satisfy two men at once, then the Junoesque Swede was surely it. Her huge, melon-like breasts were each a two-handed job in themselves, and her sturdy, muscular yet shapely body looked packed with enough sexual energy and stamina to withstand sustained fucking for a week.

Licking their lips in eager anticipation, they both followed Freda's lead by stripping down to the buff in double-quick time.

Both Wayne and Charlie already had formidable erections. Freda allowed herself a precious few moments to feast her eyes on her twin treats, congratulating herself on her excellent choice. Whilst neither cock on its own could possibly compare with John's supreme weapon, taken as a pair they packed a more than generous portion of prime meat. And Freda was feeling particularly ravenous.

Wasting no further time, she grabbed a firm hold of the two rigid pricks and guided their captive owners into their required positions, facing each other on either side of the massage table. Then, after carefully adjusting the height of the table to suit her plans, Freda draped herself belly-down across it. She wriggled her body forward until she could just slide her parted lips over the head of Wayne's rampant manhood and shook her arse invitingly at Charlie.

It was an invitation difficult to resist, and being a wise man, Charlie didn't even try. Moving up behind her, he jumped eagerly forward between Freda's parted legs, cupping his hands under her meaty thighs. Lifting and pulling them apart, Charlie guided the head of his dancing cock between the soft cheeks of her delicious arse to the succulent mouth of her welcoming cunt. A single push was all it took to ease his stiff prick deep into her cavernous tunnel, sliding smoothly up the slippery walls until he was buried up to the hilt.

Freda let out a deep and guttural grunt of satisfaction, craning her neck forward to gulp more of Wayne's love-poker into her mouth. Satisfactorily filled with stiff cock at both ends, the Swedish Amazon began rocking herself to and fro across the massage table, using her well-honed stomach muscles to maximum advantage.

Quickly establishing a smooth, fluid movement and a regular rhythm, Freda became a precision fucking and sucking machine. As she backed on to Charlie's stiff prick, her soft lips would glide up Wayne's hot shaft, allowing her to briefly lick the swollen head with her agile tongue. Then, on the return, she would pull herself off Charlie's meaty spike and gobble at Wayne's prick as it filled her eager mouth again.

Using her athletic prowess to the full, the big Swedish girl's body was a blur of movement as she satisfied her frenzied lust on two fat cocks. From her mouth to her cunt, she was a pure animal, writhing with naked and savage sexual energy. Wayne and Charlie had little to do but stand there as their pricks were alternately swallowed and then spat out again by two hungry, sucking holes.

Freda's fluid rhythm started to falter, becoming more jerky and erratic as her orgasm rose within her. Beginning to feel the desperate need for release, she concentrated more on the cravings of her yearning cunt, pushing herself back on to the full length of Charlie's intruding cock and rolling her great arse around its thick shaft. Gasping for breath, she was no longer able to suck Wayne's prick with quite so much loving attention, contenting herself with merely lashing it with her tongue whenever she could reach it.

Disgruntled by this second-rate treatment, Wayne took matters into his own hands. Twining his fingers into Freda's blonde tresses, he pulled her head towards him and jabbed his cock deep into her throat. Slurping greedily upon it and snorting through her nose, she redoubled her efforts to suck the inner juices from him.

Charlie was putting a bit of effort in himself now, as his excitement rose to fever pitch. Pulling on Freda's thighs, he bucked his hips furiously as he rammed into the Swedish girl's brimming honeypot. Being energetically fucked at both ends finally destroyed any rhythm or grace in her movements. Freda's body jerked and jumped on the massage table as the two men pumped her mouth and cunt respectively.

Wayne came first, spurting his creamy emission into Freda's hungry mouth. Pressing her lips tightly around the throbbing shaft, she rolled the tangy sperm briefly around with her tongue before gulping it down greedily. Opening her mouth and pulling her head back slightly, she let out a long, shuddering moan of pleasure.

The taste of come in her throat was the final trigger to send Freda into the first spasms of orgasm. Rolling her lovely arse around furiously, she clenched her internal muscles around Charlie's thrusting cock. She enjoyed one last, savage thrust against her buttocks and then the delicious sensation of Charlie's thick cock throbbing away inside her as he shot his bolt overcame her.

Whimpering with sheer ecstasy and exhaustion, Freda lay limply across the massage table and gasped for breath as Wayne and Charlie pulled their dripping pricks out of her mouth and cunt and stood back grinning happily at each other.

'What you reckon, Charlie?' Wayne muttered thoughtfully, after a while. 'Give ourselves a couple of minutes to recover and try it again the other way round?'

Charlie nodded enthusiastically. 'Bloody right,' he agreed. 'I reckon I could keep this up all night.'

Chapter Nineteen

The next two weeks passed in a blur of frenetic activity. Amanda saw less and less of Miles as he got deeper and deeper into the film, shooting every day and spending most of his nights in the cutting room. To her surprise, she found that she missed his company, and was looking forward to sharing some time with him when Sunday came round.

Arriving in the breakfast room shortly before nine o'clock, she noted with some dismay that the full crew were already there and dressed in their working clothes. Obviously, film-making was a seven-day-a-week occupation, she thought.

Seating herself at Miles' table, Amanda was unable to hide the disappointment on her face.

'Why so glum?' Miles wanted to know.

Amanda sighed deeply. 'Filming today as well? I thought you'd be taking Sunday off.'

Miles shook his head, mumbling through a mouthful of toast. 'Can't afford to waste a day, I'm afraid. Not now the film's almost finished. Why, thinking of going to church, were you?'

Amanda pouted sulkily. 'Not exactly,' she told him. 'Although I had hoped I might get in a little private worship at the temple of the great god Priapus.'

Miles looked apologetic. 'Sorry, Amanda, I really am,' he murmured. 'But perhaps I can find time to be with you this evening.'

'That's bloody generous of you,' Amanda muttered, unable to keep sarcasm out of her voice. It might be the best offer she was going to get, she realised – but she didn't have to look happy about it.

Miles noted her obvious annoyance and decided on a concession.

'Look, you can join me on the set if you like,' he suggested. 'Then, when I've set everything up and the cameras are rolling, perhaps we can sneak off for an hour or so.'

It was a compromise which Amanda was happy to accept. Her face brightened, as she thought of all the different sexual configurations which could be fitted into a single hour. Andrew came round serving coffee, and Amanda accepted a cup.

'How come you're serving breakfast?' she asked in surprise. 'Where's Sally?'

Andrew bent over her, whispering in a conspiratorial fashion. 'She won't come out because of Emily,' he confided. 'She's afraid the bloody woman is going to suddenly blurt out her total and undying love for the whole damned room to hear.'

Amanda looked surprised. In all the time she had known Andrew and Sally, she had never seen either of them embarrassed about anything sexual. 'Wouldn't have thought that sort of thing could possibly worry a pair of old swingers like you two,' she observed.

Andrew nodded miserably. 'Normally it wouldn't,' he

admitted. 'But Sally feels guilty about involving the poor girl in one of her little schemes, and now she's totally strung out about the whole thing. Bloody nuisance all round, really. It means I have to do twice as much work.'

Having aired his moans, Andrew slunk off, leaving Miles and Amanda together.

'So, what's on the script for today?' she enquired chattily, sipping at her coffee.

Miles grinned. 'Another red letter day for Big John,' he told her. 'He finally gets to bonk Shelley in a bubble-bath. I think she's rather looking forward to it herself.'

Amanda smiled a secretive little smile. 'Tell her to bring plenty of shower gel,' she murmured mysteriously, remembering her own experience with John's oversized equipment.

Reading between the lines, Miles chose not to pursue the matter. He finished off his last piece of toast, drained his coffee cup and jumped to his feet.

'Well, everyone to work,' he announced to the whole room. 'We have a heavy schedule today.'

There were a few half-hearted groans of protest, but it seemed the entire crew were good-natured about working on a Sunday. Amanda trotted meekly behind Miles as he led them all out of the breakfast room.

Amanda had wondered how Miles was going to set up a bathtub scene in the gymnasium, and now she knew. The bath, complete with a full load of hot sudsy water, was already in position, surrounded on three sides by a painted backdrop. The bath itself looked rather familiar, Amanda thought. Very similar to the colour-matched sanitary ware which she had had fitted throughout the club bedrooms, in fact.

Miles caught her staring at it and smiled sheepishly.
'Yes, hope you don't mind,' he muttered apologetically.
'It's out of my room. I had Wayne and Charlie disconnect
it first thing this morning. Only don't worry – everything
will all be put back just as it was before we leave, and any
damage will come out of the budget.'

Presented with such a *fait accompli*, there wasn't much
Amanda could say. She consoled herself with the thought
that it might be useful to know a couple of handy
plumbers in case of a future emergency. She backed to the
side of the gym, moving out of the way as Miles scurried
about getting the equipment set up as he wanted it, and
making sure everyone was in place.

Everything was finally ready and the cameras were set to
roll. Miles despatched Emily to make up John and Shelley
and bring them on set. She returned five minutes later
with the two stars, both of whom were grinning like Chesh-
ire cats. John was wearing only his underpants and Shelley's flimsy negligee looked extremely creased. Something
told Amanda that they had been doing a bit of private
rehearsal.

Miles took them both aside for a last-minute run-
through.

'You understand what we're doing today?' he queried,
first of all. 'This is a straight follow-through from the scene
we filmed the other day. If you remember, you'd both just
finished making love to your respective partners and decided to have a bath. You both come out of your rooms at
the same time, meet unexpectedly in the corridor and
immediately fancy each other like hell. Now you've decided to have a little orgy in the bath together.' Miles

paused, glancing questioningly at each of them in turn. 'So, have you got it?' he asked, finally.

John nodded. 'Got it,' he confirmed.

'Good, so we'll take it from there,' Miles said. 'We start filming as you and Shelley come in to the bathroom.'

He turned to address the crew. 'OK, we're all set for a take,' he announced. 'So . . . lights . . . cameras . . . action.'

Miles retreated to join Amanda as filming began. 'How's about us taking that little break we promised ourselves?' he suggested, smiling.

The sparkle in Amanda's eye was answer enough. Clutching her hand, Miles began to lead her towards the exit.

'Hold everything,' Emily suddenly bawled out at the top of her voice. 'We've got a continuity error here.'

The smile was wiped from Miles' face abruptly. 'Shit,' he cursed, under his breath. He glanced at Amanda apologetically. 'Sorry, love – just a temporary glitch to sort out.' Leaving her, he strode over to Emily, who was scanning her continuity script with a deep frown on her face.

'What's the problem?' Miles asked her.

Emily nodded towards John. 'Underpants,' she muttered briskly. 'They're the wrong colour.'

Miles regarded her blankly. 'What's wrong with them?'

'They're blue,' Emily pointed out. 'But according to my notes he was wearing red underpants when we shot the preceding scene. So how do we explain that his underwear miraculously seems to have changed colour in the middle of the night?'

It was a good question, Miles thought. The problem was, he didn't have a good answer. 'Shit,' he said again, with a whole volume of emotion behind the single word. It was not a good time to have a problem. Not when you had an extremely randy young woman waiting for you and who was now starting to look extremely peeved.

Frustrated, he took his anger out on John. 'Dammit, John – have you changed your fucking underpants?' he yelled out, making the question sound more like an accusation.

John glared back at him indignantly. 'Of course I've changed my bloody pants. I change 'em every day. Doesn't everyone?'

'Well where are the red ones?' Miles demanded.

John shrugged his shoulders. 'I threw them in the dirty linen basket in my bedroom,' he answered. 'But as far as I know they haven't come back from the laundry yet.'

Miles was becoming increasingly irritated. He looked over at Amanda. 'Is that right?'

Amanda nodded. 'Afraid so, Miles. Tuesdays and Fridays are laundry delivery days.'

Fuming now, Miles turned back to John again. 'Well have you got another red pair?' he demanded.

John shook his head. 'White ones, blue ones – and I think I have an old pair of green ones – but no red ones.'

'Why can't we just send someone out to buy a new pair?' Emily suggested helpfully. 'The budget will stretch to that, surely?'

Miles shot her a withering look. 'And where the hell do you suggest we buy men's underpants in the wilds of the countryside on a Sunday morning?' he wanted to know. 'A car boot sale, perhaps? The garden fete at the local vicarage?'

Emily fell silent, wishing she'd kept her mouth shut about the underpants business in the first place. It was highly doubtful that anyone who watched porno movies was likely to be that observant, let alone even remotely interested in the finer points of film continuity.

'I've got an idea,' John put in brightly. 'Why don't I simply put in a little bit of extra dialogue to explain things. For instance, I could say something like "Oh by the way, I had some come-stains on my red underpants, so I changed them."'

Miles groaned aloud. 'Oh, that's fucking rich, that is,' he exploded bitterly. 'You're alone with a raving nymphomaniac who wants to fuck you in a bathtub and you're going to turn her on by telling her about your come-stained pants. Real erotic stuff, that.'

In mounting desperation, he turned on Franklin. 'You're the costume expert – so how about finding some red material and knocking up a quick pair of Y-fronts on your sewing machine?'

The little man tossed his head disdainfully. 'Well, I suppose I *could*,' he said grudgingly. 'Although it's hardly the sort of thing a creative artiste of my calibre should be doing with his talents.' He paused, glancing aside at John with a sly look in his eyes. 'Of course, I'd have to take the proper measurements.'

'Will you fuck,' John growled at him aggressively. 'You dangle your measuring tape anywhere near my crotch and I'll bloody well use it to strangle you.'

Franklin paled, a little shiver running through his slight frame. 'Oh dear, he's a bit butch, isn't he?' he complained to Miles. 'I don't think I can do anything with him.'

Miles had taken enough. He finally blew his cool. Pushing past Franklin, he marched over to John. 'Right – get those bloody pants off,' he snapped testily.

The man was not in a mood to argue with, John thought. He did as he was told, peeling off his blue underpants and handing them to Miles.

Holding them gingerly between his thumb and finger, Miles carried them over to Franklin and stuffed them into his hands. 'Here, use these as a pattern and make a matching pair in red,' he commanded. 'And if you can't find any red material just cut your fucking throat and bleed over them for five minutes.'

Franklin considered throwing a little tantrum and decided against it. With another little toss of his head, he flounced off, speaking over his shoulder. 'It'll take about twenty minutes.'

Miles let his shoulders slump, letting out a long, slow sigh as he tried to relax. 'Well, thank Christ that's sorted out,' he announced, to no-one in particular.

He strode back to join Amanda, forcing an apologetic smile. 'Well, sorry love, but you heard what the man said. Twenty minutes. Doesn't give us much time, does it?'

'Then we'll just have to make it a quickie,' Amanda said, grabbing hold of his hand and dragging him towards the fire exit. She pushed open the emergency release bar and flung the doors open, slamming them closed again behind her. Safely locked outside, she thrust Miles against the back wall and dived straight for the front of his fly, grasping his zipper between her fingers and tugging it down in a flash.

Before Miles was really sure what was happening, Amanda had slid his trousers down to his knees and hooked his prick out of his underpants. Cupping it in her hand, she dropped to her knees and wrapped her lips around the soft flesh.

Miles gulped, casting his eyes about from side to side and looking rather panicky. 'Christ, Amanda – we can't just do it right out here in the open,' he protested weakly.

Amanda let his cock pop out of her mouth for just long enough to answer him. 'Relax, Miles – no-one ever comes round here to the back of the club.' She got straight back to the job in hand, swallowing his prick again and sucking on it furiously.

Despite his reservations, Miles felt his cock swell rapidly as Amanda treated it to the full and expert attention of her lips, mouth and tongue. Finally getting it fully stiff, Amanda ran her tongue up and down the full throbbing length a couple of times then jumped to her feet. Reaching up under her skirt, she pulled down her panties and kicked them off. Holding the front of her skirt up again, she stepped forward, spread the lips of her cunt aside with her fingers and climbed onto his upright cock.

'There we are – the quickest quickie in the sex manual,' she announced, thrusting her hips forward so that his prick slipped into the creamy recesses of her love-tunnel.

Then, bracing herself with her hands spread flat against the wall, Amanda flexed her knees and began to ride up and down his fleshy pole like a monkey on a stick. It was not the most graceful of sexual positions, but it was reasonably comfortable and satisfying, and it was not long before Amanda felt her juices flowing within her.

Pinned back against the wall, there was little Miles could do except lean back and enjoy the delightful sensation of

Amanda's tight cunt gliding up and down the length of his cock. Excited by the suddenness and urgency of her passion, and the added faint thrill of danger that he felt about making love in the open air, he reached the point of orgasm in a matter of a couple of minutes.

Feeling him shudder as he spurted his passion inside her cunt, Amanda speeded up her efforts to achieve her own release before his stiff cock wilted. She humped herself up and down frantically until she felt a satisfying shivery feeling in her gut, and the first orgasmic wavelets rippling from her loins into her thighs.

It was not the most spectacular of orgasms, but Amanda was more than satisfied. With a low, shuddering sigh of contentment rather than a gasp of pleasure, Amanda pushed herself deep onto Miles' cock one last time and held him inside her as her cunt throbbed around it. She flopped against him as his manhood melted away inside her.

Satisfaction achieved, she stepped back, picked up her panties from the ground and pulled them back on again.

'Well, was that quick enough for you?' she enquired of Miles with a little smirk on her face.

Miles grinned sheepishly as he reached down for his trousers. 'You're an extremely brazen woman, Miss Redfern. You took undue and lustful advantage of me,' he accused her jokingly. 'You now owe me one long, slow and exceedingly comfortable screw – and I fully intend to collect it at the earliest opportunity.'

'A debt I shall be only too happy to repay,' Amanda assured him fervently. She glanced down as he slipped his limp cock back into his pants and suddenly started to giggle stupidly.

'What the hell's up with you?' Miles asked, starting to zip up his trousers with a slight frown forming on his face.

Amanda was unable to answer him for several seconds, finally getting control of herself and assuming a more or less straight face. She reached out and tugged down the zipper he had just pulled up.

Misinterpreting her actions, Miles pulled back defensively as Amanda curled her fingers inside the waistband of his pants. 'Oh no – not again,' he said firmly.

Amanda shook her head, giggling again. 'I just wanted to show you something,' she told him, stretching the material of his pants out through his fly.

Miles glanced down, suddenly looking and feeling rather stupid as he saw what Amanda was trying to point out to him.

'I'm wearing red bloody underpants,' he muttered, making a rather superfluous observation.

The sense of annoyance he felt with himself for the lost time faded quickly as Amanda's humour infected him. Letting out a short, rueful laugh, he shrugged his shoulders carelessly. 'Oh well, I suppose the time wasn't entirely wasted,' he said philosophically, slipping his arm around Amanda's waist. 'And it gave Franklin something to do.'

Cuddling each other and laughing, they headed back around the side of the building towards the gymnasium.

Franklin had already returned with the makeshift pair of underpants, which he had managed to cobble up from one of his best silk shirts. This was something which he was at great pains to point out as he handed them to Miles, who did not appear suitably impressed. Muttering heavily beneath his breath about his favourite Italian designer, Franklin hovered on the brink of a major tantrum as Miles passed the flimsy garment on to John.

John's reaction was equally dismissive. Waving them in the air, he sniffed in a faint gesture of disgust. 'They look more like a pair of bloody ladies knickers than a pair of underpants,' he complained bitterly.

Miles was in no mood to cope with any further carping from either of them. 'Just get them on until I tell you to get 'em off again,' he snapped. He turned his attention to Franklin. 'And if I hear so much as another murmur from you, I'll go through your entire fucking wardrobe with a pair of pinking shears,' he threatened.

Satisfied that he had staved off a minor mutiny, Miles redirected his attention to the film crew.

'Right, after all that fucking about, could we just get on with finishing off this bloody movie?' he asked wearily.

Chapter Twenty

Amanda lay in bed, listening to the faint sounds of the film crew loading up their vehicles in the drive beneath her window. She felt a sense of anti-climax, almost depression, to realise that it was all over. The film was as good as completed, with only the final dubbing to be done. It had been a wild but exhilarating three weeks, but now it was finished. It was time to return to the real world, Amanda realised.

It was this feeling as much as anything which had made her decide to stay in bed. Although part of her wanted to say goodbye to everyone, and see them on their way, there was another part which told her that it might not be a good idea. She remembered something Miles had said to her. 'Films aren't *real*, Amanda – and perhaps even the people connected with them aren't real either.'

So perhaps it was better to stay out of the way, she had told herself. Just let the three-week fantasy evaporate away like a dream upon waking. If Miles wanted to see her before he left, he knew where she was. At the mere thought of the man, there was an aching feeling deep in the pit of her belly.

There was a gentle tap on the door at that very moment. 'Amanda?' she heard Miles call softly. 'It's me, Miles.'

Amanda's heart gave a little jump. 'Come on in, the door's unlocked,' she called out eagerly. She sat up in bed, letting the thin coverlet fall away from her naked body as the door began to open.

Miles stepped into the room, a slightly sad little smile on his face. Running his eyes over Amanda's beautiful coral-tipped breasts, he sighed deeply.

'Come to say goodbye, have you?' Amanda asked, sensing his mood.

A twinkle of humour returned to Miles' eyes. 'Well, not really,' he murmured. 'It was more of a debt-collecting call, actually.'

Amanda looked slightly perplexed, so Miles explained. 'That long slow comfortable screw you owe me?' he reminded her. 'I thought now might be a good time for us to settle up.'

Amanda smiled wistfully. 'There couldn't be a better time,' she agreed. 'And I'm a girl who likes to pay her debts in full.' To emphasise the point, she threw the bed-cover back completely, exposing the full lushness of her ripe young body.

Miles had already started to take off his clothes. Finally stripping his shirt off over his head, he stood there completely naked.

'I see you came prepared,' Amanda observed with a throaty chuckle, regarding his already tumescent prick with unconcealed admiration.

Miles grinned, stepping across the room towards her. He knelt across her thighs, facing her. Pressing his manly chest against the soft warmth of her beautiful tits, he kissed her passionately, running the tip of his hot tongue around the outline of her lips. He opened his mouth as she responded instantly, sending her own tongue darting between his teeth like a wet snake.

Amanda wrapped her arms around his back, hugging him against her and feeling the hardness of his cock pressing against the softness of her belly. Letting her head flop back onto the sumptuous pillows, she pulled him down on top of her. They kissed again, exploring each other's mouths with their tongues.

Despite his throbbing hardness, Amanda could sense that Miles was not in the mood for desperate and hurried lovemaking. His kisses were sensuous rather than passionate, and he seemed relaxed, wanting no more for the moment than gentle love-play.

She was more than happy to oblige. Taking hold of his hands, Amanda pressed them against the sides of her swelling tits.

No man could possibly resist the chance of two such delicious handfuls. Raising himself into a kneeling position again, Miles cupped the palms of his hands over both lush, creamy mounds and massaged them gently with his fingers. He turned his attention to her nipples, toying with them lovingly. Pinching each soft pink bud gently, he rolled them between his thumb and forefinger until they hardened to stiff little peaks.

Amanda sighed softly, knowing now that Miles was going to exact his debt to the very letter of the law. A long slow comfortable screw he had been promised, and a long slow comfortable screw he was going to take. It was an agreement that she was more than happy to honour. She reached up to clasp her hands around the back of his neck, pulling his head down towards her breasts.

Miles buried his face gratefully between the jutting, swelling mounds, enjoying their soft elasticity. Smelling the musky sweetness of Amanda's body, he wanted to taste it, and sucked and licked at her vibrant flesh with his lips and tongue. Clamping his mouth over one breast, he took the nipple between his teeth, nibbling gently at the juicy titbit. Releasing it again, he teased it with his slithering wet tongue before transferring his attentions to its waiting twin.

Amanda moaned softly as his oral ministrations sent warm and pulsing ripples of pleasure through her entire body. She shuffled her body and wriggled her hips until she felt the soft weight of his swollen balls settle between her thighs and against the moist lips of her cunt. Reaching for his rampant cock, she stroked it like a favourite pet, grinning with delight as it jerked under her touch.

It was time to start making love in earnest, Miles realised. He slid down her body, allowing his stiff cock to drop between her thighs. Amanda responded eagerly, grasping the stiff tube in her hand and guiding it between the soft lips of her labia. Rubbing it gently up and down her hot little slit, she made sure the head was well-coated with pussy-juice before wiggling it into final position.

Miles pushed gently, easing his cock into the moist heat of her inviting cleft. With the first two or three inches well engaged, he completed the remainder of the journey with a single thrust of his hips, driving the full length of his love-machine into her receptive tunnel.

Amanda received the generous offering with a low moan of delight. She spread her thighs, kicking her legs out convulsively as she felt the meaty rod surge inside her.

Reaching round behind his buttocks, she clenched her fingers against the firm flesh and pulled him against her.

Mindful of his needs, Amanda contracted the muscles of her vaginal walls, clamping his cock inside her. It was a little trick she had learned many years ago, and was usually brought into play for her own benefit, to speed up her own orgasm. Now, however, it was to excite Miles without over-stimulating him too quickly.

It seemed to work. Miles groaned with pleasure as the soft and hot walls of Amanda's cunt seemed to close around his prick like a gloved hand, gripping it in a loving embrace. It was a totally sensuous and thrilling sensation, and Miles had the fanciful idea that somehow Amanda's fanny had a life of its own, an independent existence. Certainly it seemed that his cock was being pulled and sucked into a moving, flowing tunnel which tickled, kissed and caressed the taut flesh in a way that he had never imagined possible. More than content to make the delicious feeling last as long as possible, he lay almost still, making no more than an occasional soft thrust with his belly muscles.

Amanda continued milking his prick with her magical cunt, desperately holding back the onset of her orgasm. Although she actually longed for Miles to slam his rod deep into her belly, she had made a pact and intended to keep it, even if she had to make certain sacrifices herself. She could only hope that sooner or later Miles would feel the need for release himself and they could both abandon themselves to the kind of wild animal fucking which gave her the greatest pleasure.

Strangely, it never happened and Amanda found she didn't miss it. Miles came suddenly and unexpectedly, with no more than a surprised little grunt. His knees tightened convulsively against the sides of Amanda's thighs, and he kissed her again with deep and savage passion.

She felt his juice flow, rather than spurt into her womb, and it somehow set the seal on this, their final lovemaking. Amanda threw her arms around his broad back, hugging him close. Then, with something approaching a sob rising in her throat, she released her own orgasm in a long, slow and trickling flood.

They lay silently together for nearly an hour afterwards, as though both of them feared to speak first, thus accepting or even precipitating their inevitable parting.

It was Amanda who first broke the silence, voicing the question uppermost in her mind.

'Will I ever see you again?' she asked, as though it was nothing more than a polite enquiry.

There was a puzzled, almost accusing expression on Miles' face as he turned towards her. 'Christ, Amanda – didn't you understand what I was trying to say to you when I told you that you and I weren't part of a film?' he murmured. 'Besides, do you really think I could have discovered a place like Paradise and never want to come back again?'

Miles was silent again for a moment, a slightly mischievous grin forming on his face. 'Anyway, I might want to return and shoot a sequel,' he told her.

Amanda wasn't sure whether he was joking or not. 'Really?' she asked, cautiously.

Miles was serious again now as he answered her.

'Oh yes,' he said. 'Didn't you know? There's always a sequel.'

Headline Delta Erotic Survey

In order to provide the kind of books you like to read – and to qualify for a free erotic novel of the Editor's choice – we would appreciate it if you would complete the following survey and send your answers, together with any further comments, to:

> Headline Book Publishing
> FREEPOST (WD 4984)
> London
> NW1 0YR

1. Are you male or female?
2. Age? Under 20 / 20 to 30 / 30 to 40 / 40 to 50 / 50 to 60 / 60 to 70 / over
3. At what age did you leave full-time education?
4. Where do you live? (Main geographical area)
5. Are you a regular erotic book buyer / a regular book buyer in general / both?
6. How much approximately do you spend a year on erotic books / on books in general?
7. How did you come by this book?
7a. If you bought it, did you purchase from: a national bookchain / a high street store / a newsagent / a motorway station / an airport / a railway station / other . . .
8. Do you find erotic books easy / hard to come by?
8a. Do you find Headline Delta erotic books easy / hard to come by?
9. Which are the best / worst erotic books you have ever read?
9a. Which are the best / worst Headline Delta erotic books you have ever read?
10. Within the erotic genre there are many periods, subjects and literary styles. Which of the following do you prefer:
10a. (period) historical / Victorian / C20th / contemporary / future?
10b. (subject) nuns / whores & whorehouses / Continental frolics / s&m / vampires / modern realism / escapist fantasy / science fiction?

10c. (styles) hardboiled / humorous / hardcore / ironic / romantic / realistic?

10d. Are there any other ingredients that particularly appeal to you?

11. We try to create a cover appearance that is suitable for each title. Do you consider them to be successful?

12. Would you prefer them to be less explicit / more explicit?

13. We would be interested to hear of your other reading habits. What other types of books do you read?

14. Who are your favourite authors?

15. Which newspapers do you read?

16. Which magazines?

17 Do you have any other comments or suggestions to make?

If you would like to receive a free erotic novel of the Editor's choice (available only to UK residents), together with an up-to-date listing of Headline Delta titles, please supply your name and address. Please allow 28 days for delivery.

Name ....

Address ....

....

....

A selection of Erotica from Headline